WOLF

The Exiled 2

Lynn Hagen

**EVERLASTING CLASSIC
MANLOVE**

**Siren Publishing, Inc.
www.SirenPublishing.com**

A SIREN PUBLISHING BOOK
IMPRINT: Everlasting Classic ManLove

WOLF
Copyright © 2012 by Lynn Hagen

ISBN: 978-1-62242-098-8

First Printing: November 2012

Cover design by Les Byerley
All art and logo copyright © 2012 by Siren Publishing, Inc.

Printed in the U.S.A.

PUBLISHER
Siren Publishing, Inc.
www.SirenPublishing.com

WOLF

The Exiled 2

LYNN HAGEN
Copyright © 2012

Chapter One

"What the hell." Jaycee groaned as his car sputtered and then died. He carefully veered the vehicle to the curb as he began to curse up a storm, smacking the steering wheel in his angry tirade. He couldn't believe this was happening to him. "You're not supposed to die. I just had you fixed." He was practically whining at the hunk of junk as if it would sympathize with him and start up. He wasn't holding his breath for that miracle, but it would have been nice.

Jaycee had to scrape the money together for the repairs in the first place, and now this? There was no way he was working another three weeks of overtime for repair costs. His car was not getting another damn dime out of him.

Frustrated, he climbed out of the car and walked around back, kicking the back tire in frustration. "Now what am I supposed to do?"

He really wasn't looking for his car to answer him, but yelling out loud made him feel better.

Somewhat.

Feeling irritated that his only mode of transportation was now an oversized paperweight, Jaycee reached in the car, pulled the hood lever, and then walked around to see what the problem was. As he held the hood up, he wondered what he was doing. He hadn't a clue what he was looking at. What did he know about cars?

Not a damn thing. But for some reason, looking under the hood made him feel like a solution was going to pop out at him.

But it didn't. He stared at a dirty motor and hadn't a clue what was what. The only thing that looked familiar to him was the plastic container sitting off to the side of the engine that he poured washer fluid into occasionally.

Growling, he let the hood drop back into place, hearing it smack closed as he walked around to the passenger side and grabbed his backpack from the front seat. It was only three blocks to the house he shared with two other men. It shouldn't take him too long to get home on foot.

Thankfully he was on his way home from work instead of the other way around. His boss was an asshole, and Jaycee hated to deal with the man on any basis.

As he glanced at his car, Jaycee really didn't want to leave it behind, but it was parked at the curb. There shouldn't be any problem, unless one of the neighbors called to report an abandoned car outside their home.

Gods, he hoped not. He didn't need for his POS to be towed. That would only be another bill he couldn't afford, and he wasn't going to sink another dime into it. Jaycee contemplated leaving a note on the front windshield to let everyone know that he would be back for his car, but then that would also tell people that it was a heap of metal just sitting there.

Maybe he could find someone to give him a jump later. Rico had a car. His roommate would probably help out, but with Rico, one never knew.

Deciding against alerting anyone that his car was not running, Jaycee hiked the strap of his backpack onto his shoulder and headed home. After working ten hours, he'd rather not be walking, but he didn't have any choice in the matter. His body ached and he wanted a hot shower desperately, but there wasn't anything he could do about his situation. He was stuck walking, so he needed to stop mentally bitching about it and get moving if he ever wanted to get home. Pulling his iPod out, he shoved the earbuds in his ears and turned the music on.

As he rounded the corner of the second block, Jaycee noticed a man leaning against a tree close to the curb. The man was just leaning there. It should have been no big deal. Maybe the guy was waiting for someone to pick him up. But the hairs on the back of Jaycee's neck stood on end as he walked closer to the stranger.

He tried to keep his eyes averted, but he could still feel the man's stare boring into him. It was seriously creeping him out. Jaycee reached into his pocket and turned the music down once he passed the guy. He wasn't sure why, but something told him he needed to be on full alert and aware of his surroundings.

There was just something not right about the stranger leaning against the tree. Maybe it was all the dark clothes the stranger was wearing, or possibly the badass attitude the guy was projecting. Whatever it was, Jaycee heard the vibes loud and clear.

Stay away.

Jaycee picked up his pace a tad, suppressing the urge to full-out run. He was probably overreacting, and most likely was. He'd been known to freak out before. Jaycee was the type to freak the hell out first and then think things through once he had a meltdown. It was a flaw of his, one his mom tried to break him of for years, but Jaycee was who he was.

Just because he tended to react first and think later didn't mean he was going to ignore the feeling that danger was somewhere near. The feeling was like a wet blanket over him, making him aware of everything around him as the heavy, oppressing sensation of someone following him weighed him down.

As his house came into view, Jaycee let out a relieved breath.

He had been overreacting.

Figures.

He had let his imagination take flight and scare him into thinking that someone was after him. The man was no threat to him. He was almost home, and the stranger was nowhere in sight. Jaycee felt stupid for getting all worked up over nothing.

His roommates always teased Jaycee that he had an overactive imagination. They said he scared easily and could turn something ordinary into a big hoopla. Jaycee had argued that they were the ones overreacting, but maybe they were right. He chuckled to himself, feeling like a total dweeb. What did he think would happen next, the Secret Service would pull up and kidnap him?

Okay, so he had an overactive imagination. Sue him. It kept life from being boring, and there was nothing Jaycee hated more than being bored. And unfortunately, right now, his life was about as boring as it could get. He wasn't a thrill seeker, but a little more action wouldn't hurt to shake things up a bit.

As he headed up the driveway, going around to the back of the house, Jaycee felt his backpack being ripped away from his shoulder. He spun around to see the stranger who had been leaning against the tree standing there snarling at him.

Snarling? Who the hell snarled like a dog? It wasn't normal. No human being should be able to make that sound. Jaycee knew this was *not* his imagination in overdrive. This guy was real, and looking as if he was about to take a big chunk out of Jaycee's hide.

Jaycee's eyes widened as fear wrapped its claws tightly around his chest when he saw how utterly black the man's eyes were. The irises looked like fathomless orbs that could suck him in if he stared too long. No one's eyes should be that dark. The irises blended with the pupils, making it hard for Jaycee to tell where one ended and the other began.

The stranger also had long, sharp teeth in his mouth. They reminded Jaycee of a dog's canine teeth. The points were long, almost touching the man's lower lips, telling Jaycee that this man was something other than human. That couldn't be right. His imagination was running away with him at the wrong damn moment, but Jaycee couldn't stop the feeling that something bad was about to happen.

"What the hell are you?" he asked as he backed away, trying his best to make it to the back door without running. The door was only a few feet away, but felt like a mile in his current situation. His heart was beating so fast that Jaycee felt slightly light-headed.

The man tossed Jaycee's backpack across the lawn as he moved closer, his lips pulling up into a lecherous smile as he clasped his hands behind his back, leaning slightly forward. "You smell so damn good, human. My teeth are itching to take a bite out of you."

Human?

Was the guy serious?

Jaycee's eyes shot toward the back door, wondering if he could make a break for it before the man could reach him. The guy was pretty fucking big, and Jaycee prayed the man's weight slowed him down. Not that the guy was fat, just well built, large. He knew it was a long shot, but he had to try. What other option did he have? Jaycee wasn't a fighter. He could defend himself if he had to, but he had a feeling that no amount of sheer will was going to help him in this situation. Taking a step in the direction he wanted to go, Jaycee shot forward, praying the damn back door was unlocked.

He shouted when a searing pain shot through his arm, radiating up toward his shoulder and down his body, exploding shards of pain racking his left side. He looked down to see his shirt was torn open and there was a big gash on his arm. The injury was bleeding profusely, making Jaycee nauseous just looking at the open wound that showed tissue and bone.

His vision slightly blurred, and Jaycee just knew he was going to pass out. He *hated* the sight of blood. Tissue and bone even more. It didn't help that it was his own blood and glory hanging loose and spilling from his body.

Jaycee raced for the door in a second attempt to get away. This guy was playing for keeps, and Jaycee wasn't sure he would survive if he didn't find a way to escape. He shouted in anger and fear when the knob wouldn't turn. The door was locked! He pushed his hand into his front pocket and then remembered his key was in his backpack…halfway across the yard.

Fuck!

"There is no use running from me," the man said as he moved closer, a look of triumph showing on his face.

Jaycee felt like his life was over, as if there was no more hope left in the world. Misery unlike anything he had ever experienced before washed over him, making Jaycee want to give up and give in and let the man do whatever he wanted. Fear and doubt crept into his mind, telling Jaycee to just give himself over to the man. There was no use fighting a battle he couldn't win.

Jaycee shook his head to dispel those morose thoughts. He knew they weren't right. He knew he couldn't just throw in the towel. He didn't give up and he wasn't a quitter. So why did he feel as though all hope was lost?

His eyes locked onto the long fingernails protruding from the man's fingers and knew how he had been sliced open. They were black and sharp looking, lethal in every sense of the word and dripping with Jaycee's blood. He reached up and covered his bleeding arm, moving away from the back door, trying desperately to get to his key. He could feel the warmth of his blood seeping through his fingers and trailing down his hand, but there wasn't anything he could do until he got away.

He had been looking for a little more action in his life, but damn, this was overkill.

Jaycee was light-headed, becoming dizzy. Grey spots were spreading across his vision, making Jaycee blink repeatedly to stay alert as he spotted two even larger men coming up his driveway.

This was it.

He was about to die.

The stranger had reinforcements, and there was no way Jaycee could fight off one man, let alone three.

Jaycee felt a whimper escape his mouth as his knees began to wobble. He was going down and there was no way to stop it. He was losing too much blood. The only regret he had at that moment was not finding out who the man was and why he had attacked Jaycee. He had never done anything to anyone to warrant his own death. Well, he did lie about being sick last week so he could call off of work, but that wasn't a damn death sentence.

His boss was a prick, but not even Herbert would spend the cash to hire a hit man for a call off. Oh hell, he was babbling in his mind. That couldn't be a good sign. Jaycee blinked a few more times, trying his best to stay upright. His plan wasn't working out so well when his vision swam before his eyes.

As the new arrivals came into the backyard, one of them began fighting the stranger who had attacked Jaycee while the other headed Jaycee's way. He didn't have the energy to fight the man. Jaycee was weak and getting weaker by the second. The only thing he could do was pray his death was quick and painless. A good snap to the neck should remedy any torture, but the man heading his way was so broad and large that Jaycee doubted he was going to like this.

As darkness started to cloud his vision, Jaycee's eyes rolled to the back of his head, his body cold as ice as he began to fall toward the ground.

* * * *

Wolf caught the human before he hit the ground, pulling him close as he tried to examine the injury on the man's left arm. But Wolf didn't get too far in his examination when his entire body began buzzing and his wings started fluttering as he glanced down at the unconscious man in his arms.

Wolf couldn't believe he was holding his mate so close, someone he thought never to find.

After so many centuries of being alone, of wishing he had someone to share his lonely existence with, he finally had his mate at his side. Wolf had someone to share his life with, and someone to keep him warm in bed. It was like a dream come true. So why did he feel scared as fuck looking down at the man? This should be a joyous occasion, but the only thing he could feel at the moment was apprehension and fear.

The human's head lolled to the side as Wolf picked the stranger up into his arms, holding him close to his chest. He could see blood spreading and soaking the man's shirt, dripping from the human's arm. It was leaving his body quickly, and Wolf felt panicked that he wouldn't save his *zaterio* in time.

From the look of the wound, Wolf couldn't tell if his mate had been bitten or scratched. It could be both, but Wolf was praying that the injury was caused by the hound's claw, not his teeth. A hell dweller's bite was poisonous, lethal to humans. Wolf felt a hole forming in his chest and a heaviness fill him at the thought of losing his mate before he even got to know who the man was.

"What are you doing?" Tyson, another of the winged beasts and the man he was patrolling the streets of Pride Pack Valley with, asked after he finally stabbed the hound in his mark.

A hound could die. It wasn't impossible. They had a dark mark behind their left ear. If stabbed there, and then burned, the hound would die and return to hell. The trick was outsmarting the hound and getting a decent shot at the mark. The hounds knew their weakness and protected the area around their ear with vengeance.

"Taking strays home now?" Tyson teased as he wiped the hound's nasty black blood from his blade onto the grass and then resheathed the sharp weapon.

"Grab the hound. We don't want Theo having a fit if you burn him here," Wolf said, ignoring Tyson's question and comment. Theo was their commander's mate. Theo had argued that burning a body in town was a very bad thing.

Wolf didn't understand why it was a bad thing, but he wasn't about to argue with Nazaryth's mate over something he found trivial.

If a hound was only stabbed, and not burned afterward, the creature could get back up again. That was some scary shit. It only made him want to burn the body on sight, but he knew he couldn't. "I'll meet you at home."

"Thanks for leaving me with the dead one," Tyson grumbled.

Wolf glanced around to make sure no one was looking before he took flight. Humans couldn't see a winged beast's five-foot expansion of wings. So it would just look like a man was flying in the air. It made for some heavy conversation on a therapist's couch for anyone who spotted them.

Wolf held on to his mate tightly as he flew toward the castle built into the side of a mountain. He had to get his *zaterio* back to his home where Wolf could tend to the man's wound and keep an eye on him for any sign of fever.

If a fever developed, Wolf would know his mate was bitten.

Gods, he prayed no fever formed.

He knew that Theo had been bitten and it had taken hours for the fever to appear. But again, Theo was a shifter. It was different for everyone. His mate was human, so Wolf hadn't a clue what to expect. He could only hold out on the hope that his mate hadn't been bitten, but scratched, because if he didn't hang on to that one thread of hope, Wolf didn't have anything else to hang on to. A *zaterio* was a chosen one for a winged beast. The only mate they would ever receive. Their chosen ones were made specifically for them. If his mate didn't survive this, neither would Wolf.

Wolf knew that the chances of a human surviving a bite by a hound were slim to none.

The bites were poisonous and nasty as hell. He had witnessed what Theo had gone through. Black foam had oozed from the shifter's pores, burning anything in its wake. And the smell of brimstone and sulfur had been noxious. The poison had Theo screaming and writhing so badly that Nazaryth had to hold Theo down. That was what their commander had told them, and Wolf knew his *zaterio* wouldn't survive that. Theo was a shifter.

His mate was not.

Landing gently and easily on the balcony of the castle, Wolf walked through the palace and headed straight for his bedroom. He saw the eyes of the other winged beasts on him, curious expressions on their faces. He wasn't going to stop to answer questions. His mate needed to lie down, and Wolf needed to pace.

Pacing never helped Wolf solve anything, but it was a distraction he needed desperately right about now.

Laying the fragile human on his bed, Wolf brushed back his mate's long fringes of black hair, noticing for the first time that the man had a goatee. He also had a generous mouth, aquiline nose, and the set of his chin hinted at a stubborn streak. His fingers traced over his mate's face, taking in his straight forehead and thick eyebrows.

Wolf studied his mate a moment longer and then walked to the adjoining bathroom to grab some gauze. He took a moment to pull himself together. Wolf felt a total wreck right now. His inside were coiled so tight he just knew he would fall apart at any second. Just because he was a winged beast didn't mean he had an endless supply of strength. Even the strongest collapsed under such pressures and worries.

Blowing out a deep breath, Wolf walked back into his bedroom and carefully ripped the rest of the shirtsleeve off, checking the injury on the man's arm and seeing the long gash from shoulder to elbow. He wasn't sure if it was just a cut or if a bite was hiding somewhere in the open wound. It was horrendous looking, and Wolf had to swallow past the lump in his throat when he saw bone and tissue. The hound had done one nasty-ass number on his mate. If the bastard wasn't dead already, Wolf would have hunted him down and tortured the hound slowly.

Winding the gauze around his mate's injury, Wolf vowed to find and eradicate as many hell dwellers as he could find. They would pay for what happened to his mate, and any other innocent that had been unlucky enough to cross a dweller's path.

Wolf grabbed a chair from across the room, setting it right next to the bed, and took a seat, resting his chin on his fists as he waited to see if his *zaterio* would fever.

Now that his mate was here, the mating heat would start. It was the last thing Wolf wanted to happen right now.

Not now, not when his *zaterio* was injured.

He couldn't even think of his mate in a sexual way as he lay there possibly fighting for his life. Wolf just wished he knew which injury his *zaterio* had sustained. It would make the waiting a hell of lot easier if he knew which outcome to look for. Maybe not, especially if the man had been bitten. Gods, he was going nuts already, and the clock had just started ticking.

"Wolf?"

He heard the commander enter his bedroom behind him, but Wolf couldn't think of anything to say. He knew it was forbidden to bring a human into the castle, but the man was his *zaterio*. What else was he supposed to do?

"He was bleeding." It was the only plausible excuse he could give his commander about why he had brought a human into their home. He couldn't think straight right now, not when he was so filled with worry that he thought he would be sick. He didn't want to talk to anyone. All he wanted to do was be with his mate. Wolf's eyes locked onto the wound, seeing that the blood was seeping through the bandage, spreading over the white gauze like a hand of death, trying its best to claim what rightfully belonged to Wolf. It worried him to see that the wound wasn't healing.

"Who was bleeding, Wolf?" Nazaryth asked.

Wolf held back the sob as his eyes roamed over his mate's perfect profile. His thoughts were scattered, and he wasn't sure he could even string an intelligent answer together. "I'm not sure if he was bitten, so I have to watch him."

"Who is he, Wolf?" the commander's voice was probing, but Wolf honestly didn't care. The only things that mattered were getting his mate better and praying he wasn't bitten.

"Why have you brought a human here?" Nazaryth asked.

Wolf held his breath when he saw the bandage seeping even more blood. *This can't be good.*

"Tell me who he is."

Wolf blinked back the tears as he stared at the most handsome man he had ever seen. Would he lose him before he got to know him? "He's my *zaterio*." He felt Nazaryth's hand on his shoulder, but it wasn't in the least bit comforting. Wolf was staring down at his mate, waiting to see if he was going to die. An overwhelming sense of loss filled him at the thought of never even knowing his mate's name, hearing his voice, or being graced with his smile.

"Have you checked his wound?"

Wolf nodded. "It's a long gash on his arm, running from shoulder to elbow, but I'm not sure if he was bitten as well," he said. "But I have to watch him." If his mate was bitten, the fever could come at any time. Wolf had to be prepared to help his mate as much as possible, even though he knew the fever meant he was going to lose the precious man. He didn't want his *zaterio* to suffer in any way.

"We need to clean his wound, Wolf."

Wolf knew this, but he feared leaving the human's side. What if his mate died while he was getting what he needed to clean the wound? He couldn't chance that. His mate was human. And that thought scared the hell out of Wolf. Humans were so delicate.

"I'll get some fresh gauze and some clean water," his commander said before leaving Wolf's bedroom.

Wolf nodded, his eyes fixed on his mate's handsome face. He wanted to see his pretty eyes again, only not filled with abject fear this time. Wolf wanted to see his mate smile. He bet the man was stunning when he smiled.

He heard Nazaryth leave his bedroom. Once he knew he was alone, Wolf leaned forward and brushed his fingers over his *zaterio*'s forehead, wanting any kind of contact he could get. The man didn't move.

Wolf moved closer, sitting on the side of the bed, staring down at the one man who was chosen for him to spend all eternity with. Sadness washed through him at the thought of being alone for the rest of all times. He knew he wouldn't be able to handle that loneliness that surrounded a winged beast. It would be too much to bear after knowing that he had lost his mate. He would go mad and have to be killed. Once a beast went mad, there was no going back. But Wolf didn't care. He wanted to be with his *zaterio*, in this life, or the next.

He growled low when he saw the soaked bandage on his mate's arm. Wolf wasn't going to wait for his commander. His mate needed his wound cleaned now.

He knew he had to clean it. Wolf dashed quickly to the bathroom and grabbed a bowl from under the sink, filled it with water and grabbed a towel, and then raced back to the bedroom. He didn't want to spend one second away from the man. Wolf wanted to memorize every single feature if his mate was going to leave him.

Wolf bent at the waist, brushing his lips over his mate's forehead. "Stay with me, my *zaterio*. I promise to make you the happiest man in the world. But you have to promise not to leave me alone," he whispered and then straightened.

He began to clean his human's arm, being as gentle as he could. He heard Nazaryth come into his bedroom, but Wolf concentrated on cleaning the blood from his mate's arm. There was just so much of it. His throat was constricted from holding back the tears as his commander came forward, Theo by his side.

"I brought the paste."

Wolf stepped aside, swallowing repeatedly as Nazaryth showed Theo how to apply the healing plants to Wolf's *zaterio*'s arm. Once Theo was done, Wolf wrapped his mate's wound.

"Any signs?" Nazaryth asked. Wolf knew his commander was speaking of the fever.

"None. He holds no fever. Not yet at least." Wolf brushed his hand over his mate's head, praying to the gods that he woke up soon. He heard the two men leave quietly. Wolf took a seat and played the waiting game.

* * * *

Jaycee inhaled sharply as his eyes fluttered open, and then he whimpered. His shoulder felt like a branding iron was being pushed into the flesh. As his vision cleared of sleep, Jaycee noticed a large, high-vaulted ceiling. His bedroom did not have a high-vaulted ceiling. It had tile, and one of the tiles was stained brown from a leaky roof.

He slammed his eyes closed, afraid to move. He wasn't sure where he was, but from the feel of the soft mattress below him, he wasn't in his backyard any longer. Or in his bed either. His bed wasn't this freaking soft. Damn, he felt like he was lying on a cloud. Maybe he had died from the attack. Maybe he really was lying on a cloud. But if he had passed the pearly gates, then why in the heck did his arm hurt so badly? Wasn't pain supposed to be a distant memory now?

He got gypped.

"How do you feel, *zaterio*?"

Oh shit. Where in the hell was he? The voice he heard was thick with accent, but Jaycee could have sworn the man just called him a Cheerio. That was what it had sounded like at least. Jaycee cracked one eye open, and then the other, wondering if he was dead.

The man hovering near him was a god! He had to be. No one looked that damn good and lived here on earth. None that Jaycee had ever seen in his life. "Where am I?" he asked, his voice sounding a little scratchy. He cleared it as he tried to sit up, but winced when pain shot down his shoulder.

"You are in a place that will keep you safe."

What the hell kind of an answer was that? Jaycee glanced around the room he was in. Damn, could it get any fancier? It reminded him of a castle from the medieval days. There were rich fabrics that hung from the walls, bookcases galore, and the bed he was lying in was nothing to sneeze at. It had to have cost a mint. The four-poster bed was made from some sort of white marble with blends of grey running through it, and there were even curtains hanging from the canopy that were pulled back on both sides.

He might not have died, but from the looks of this fancy place, he wasn't in Pride Pack Valley anymore. They didn't have castles in his town.

"Where exactly am I?"

The man moved closer, sitting on the side of the bed. Jaycee scooted an inch away. He remembered the man now. Some lunatic with sharp claws had attacked Jaycee in his own backyard, and this man had come running up the driveway just as Jaycee had passed out from blood loss. Was he in the insane man's house? Was this one of the insane man's goons? Jaycee knew he had to get out of here. The guy who had attacked him wasn't right in the head. The guy was off his freaking rocker. Jaycee remembered those weird-ass eyes, too. He never wanted to see those eyes again. The man who attacked him chilled Jaycee down to his bones.

The man scooted back a little, like he knew Jaycee was afraid, and then offered a friendly smile. "Do not fear me, *zaterio*. I would never hurt you."

Jaycee curled his fingers into the blanket, wondering how quickly he could get from the bed to the door before Hercules stopped him. "Why do you keep calling me a Cheerio?"

The man's deep and rich laughter boomed through the room as his emerald-green eyes sparkled with delight. Well, at least this lunatic was gorgeous.

Wait, he shouldn't be thinking that right now. He should be thinking about getting the hell out of here. But Jaycee couldn't deny the guy was hot, and the smile only made the guy even more attractive.

When the laughter slowed, the man shook his head, looking as if he were the happiest man on earth. Jaycee couldn't understand that look. Not that he had any experience with men looking at him like that. Jaycee had known he was gay at a very early age, but no guy had ever shown any interest in him, and Jaycee had kind of gotten used to being ignored.

Living in a small town where he really didn't know too many of the residents, the pickings were slim. He had lived here his entire life, but Jaycee hadn't made many friends. He knew a few people he worked with, and his roommates, but mostly kept to himself.

But this man wasn't ignoring him.

The heat in his eyes as he stared at Jaycee told him exactly what the guy was thinking. "I am calling you *zaterio*." The man said the last word slowly, putting emphasis on each syllable and enunciating them slowly.

"Oh," Jaycee said as he glanced at the man's broad chest. That was better than being called cereal. Maybe, it all depended on what *zah-tear-e-oh* meant. Jaycee wasn't even sure he cared right now. He just wanted to get back to his home where his loony-ass roommates would make Jaycee feel normal again. He felt like he should bow or something to the man sitting on the bed. Was he some sort of king? The room sure as shit seemed like that man should be.

"Look, thanks for the Band-Aid and your hospitality, but I must be shoving off." He grinned tightly at the well-muscled man before slowly easing from the bed. He didn't want to put any unnecessary pressure on his injury. It was already throbbing with pain.

"I am truly sorry, but you cannot leave."

Jaycee spun around at the man's words, swallowing hard when he saw the tips of fangs just under the man's lip. *Oh shit.*

Chapter Two

Wolf wished he had chosen his words a little more carefully. He could see the panic in his *zaterio*'s eyes and that was the last thing he wanted, but hell if he was letting his mate walk out the door only to be attacked again. Wolf knew just how dangerous things were out there. His mate did not. So it was up to him to protect the guy from the hell dwellers. The hounds knew by now who his mate was, or at least where he lived. If his *zaterio* went home, he would only be attacked once more. And the next time, he just might be bitten.

How very tempted Wolf was to probe his mate's mind right now. But he was not going to invade the man's private thoughts and memories without being invited. It had been done to him eons ago, and Wolf still remembered the feeling of rage that the king would take such a privilege that had not been granted to him.

"What do you mean you can't let me leave?" his mate asked, shaking his head in obvious confusion.

"What is your name?" Wolf asked. If nothing else, he wanted to know his *zaterio*'s name. He had to know it. It was a need so deep that Wolf wasn't sure he could carry on a conversation until he found out.

"Jaycee."

"I am Wolf."

"You're a wolf?"

Wolf chuckled. His mate looked so damn perplexed. The situation wasn't funny, but the look on Jaycee's face was a bit comical. "No, I am not a wolf. My name is Wolf."

"Oh," Jaycee said as he scooted closer to the door. "Nice to meet you, Wolf. Now can I leave?"

Wolf sighed as he rested his arms on his thighs. His mate was going to make this complicated as hell. Why did humans always fight against what they didn't understand? Why couldn't Jaycee just accept the fact that this was where he belonged? "No."

His *zaterio*'s eyes narrowed slightly. "So if I tried to escape, you'd stop me?" Jaycee asked as he moved another inch toward the door. He wasn't sure if Jaycee was trying to be casual about the steps he took, but Wolf wasn't blind. He could see his mate trying his best to get to the door without Wolf noticing.

"You can't just walk out of here, Jaycee. Those hounds will try to attack you again. Next time they may just bite you. It isn't safe."

"Bite me?" Jaycee paled slightly. "I don't know what would happen if they bit me, but from the look on your face, that isn't a good thing."

"No, it's not." Wolf raked a hand through his hair, feeling a need to pull it out as his wings fluttered. He wanted his mate to see the inherent danger of leaving. "Theo was bitten and nearly died. You're human. You will not live through a bite from a hell dweller."

"I think I need to sit down," Jaycee said as he crawled back up on to the bed, but made sure he stayed on the opposite end, away from Wolf. His mate's complexion was slightly green. "You said *human*. You used the word *human*. Only someone who isn't human uses that word." Jaycee's words were coming out quickly, panic edging his tone. "I'm not sure I want to know what you are, or what a hell dweller is. But you called that man a hound, too. Oh god, I'm going to be sick."

Wolf hurried to his mate's side, wondering what to do for a panic attack. He'd never dealt with one before, but he thought Jaycee could be experiencing one. "Do you want a glass of water?"

Jaycee cupped the sides of his head as he shook it back and forth. "I want to go back to when it was just humans here on earth."

Wolf bristled at his mate's confession. "That's not fair."

His hands dropped and Jaycee glared at him. "Neither is being attacked or waking up in a wacky world. You try it and see how Mary Sunshine you would feel, bub."

Wolf was slightly confused about who Mary was, but he let it go. "I have lived my entire life in a *wacky world*. I'm sorry that it has touched you, but stop crying about it." His patience was growing very thin. Jaycee was looking as if Wolf had been the one responsible for everything that had happened.

He wasn't.

The only thing he could do was try and make things as pleasant as possible for his mate. And to make matters worse, now that Jaycee was out of danger, feeling better, the heat of mating was kicking in and making Wolf's skin tight and his temper irritable. His wings wouldn't fucking stop fluttering either. Winged beasts' wings fluttered when in mating heat, wanting to wrap around their *zaterios* and claim them. Wolf had a feeling it wasn't going to be easy to claim Jaycee, but he wanted to touch the man, to caress his skin to see if it was as soft as it looked. It was taking every ounce of control not to climb over to Jaycee and fuck the man back into unconsciousness.

"Crying about it?" Jaycee asked indignantly as he fisted his hands in his lap. "Oh, buddy, I can really show you crying if you want. This is child's play compared to the fit I can throw."

Wolf wasn't sure if his mate was trying to threaten him or not. The guy was confusing as hell, and he could feel a massive headache coming on. "I don't want to argue about this, Jaycee."

"Then don't." Jaycee sniffed as he scooted from the bed and walked toward the bedroom door, his head held high and his hips rocking back and forth. Not in a sashay per se, but with determination. Damn if that sexy little ass wasn't turning him on. Wolf growled and went after his mate. His cock was hard as steel right now from the flare in Jaycee's temper. The human had no clue of the heat racing through Wolf's blood right now. He wanted to shove his cock so far into Jaycee's ass that the painfully hard erection throbbed in his jeans.

"I can't let you leave."

"Then stop me." Jaycee spun around and glared up at Wolf. "Just try and stop me, Wolf. If that is your *real* name."

"Be careful what you ask for, *zaterio*," Wolf warned. He was not above grabbing his mate and putting the human over his knee. Sweat began to form on his body as he thought of spanking the man. The images were so erotic that Wolf had to blow his breath out slowly.

Too bad it didn't help.

"I still think you're calling me a damn Cheerio." Jaycee's hair flopped around his face as he cocked his head to one side. "Are you sure you're not calling me a Cheerio?"

How the hell could his mate make him incredibly mad one moment and then make him laugh the next? Wolf was perplexed as hell. Jaycee made absolutely no sense to him whatsoever. It may have to do with the fact he hadn't dealt with humans up close and personal in centuries, but Wolf had a feeling it was just Jaycee. "I am calling you *zaterio*. Of that I am sure."

Jaycee quirked a brow, eyeing Wolf as he crept closer to the door. "You can't keep me here. I'll–I'll call the cops on you."

Wolf didn't mean to laugh, but thinking of the human police coming in here to arrest him was just funny as hell. First, they would have to find the place. The winged beasts' home resided in the side of a mountain. There were only two things visible. One was a balcony, and that was covered by mist. The second was the hangar, but with the spells around the mountain, the cops would feel a compulsive need to leave at once. And Wolf would *really* like to see someone, anyone, try and take his mate from him.

That was not happening.

The mating heat shot through him like a solar flare and was crawling up his groin and setting his damn balls on fire. His cock was hard as hell, and Jaycee looked so damn good standing there that it took every ounce of self-restraint to stop him from grabbing his mate and tossing him on the bed. Jaycee had no clue how close Wolf was to doing just that.

Goddamn this heat.

"Why would you want to leave?" Wolf asked as he spread his arms wide, ignoring the raging war going on inside his body. "This place has everything you could ever want in a home." Including him.

"Because it's not *my* home," Jaycee pointed out as his left foot slid back, taking him closer to the door. "Dude, I don't even know you from Jack."

"Who the hell is Jack?" Wolf asked with a slight growl as he took a step forward, feeling his beast wanting to unleash itself on this so-called *Jack* person. Jaycee was his *zaterio* and no one was taking the human away from him. "Is he someone I need to—" Wolf took a step back, taking in a deep breath of air. *That's it.* It was official. Either the mating heat was going to do him in, or Jaycee was. Both were driving him batty as fuck!

"It's a phrase," Jaycee said as he cocked his head to the side, wisps of black hair fringing his face as he stared at Wolf cautiously. Wolf did not want to see the look of fear and hesitation on his mate's face. He wasn't trying to frighten the man, but gods if the man wasn't getting it. It wasn't safe out there in the first place for humans, but now that the hounds new about Jaycee, the man didn't stand a chance. What part of that didn't he get? "There is no Jack, Wolf."

Wolf nodded. He was out of his depth here. He didn't know what to do or say that would make his *zaterio* stay. After centuries of isolation, he needed charm and seduction. Too bad he was clueless. He was never into head games. Wolf just wanted his mate. He didn't want to rely on charm and seduction. He just wanted Jaycee to want him.

Was that so hard?

"Look, this has been fun," Jaycee said as he slid his feet across the marble floor, bringing him even closer to the doorway. "But I have to go to work in the morning. So if you don't mind, I'm just going to hit the road."

Wolf felt helpless. It was something he didn't care to feel. He was a damn winged beast. Helpless was not something he was accustomed to feeling. But he knew he couldn't force Jaycee to stay. Any kind of force would void the claiming. If he made Jaycee afraid of him, and his mate said no when Wolf tried to claim him, the bond wouldn't form.

He was so screwed.

He also had two days to claim Jaycee before he went mad. This was not shaping up to be one of his better days.

* * * *

Okay. From what Jaycee was grasping here, Wolf wasn't one of the bad guys. Maybe. The jury was still out on that one. But that didn't mean he was staying. He wasn't born yesterday. This may be a perfect place to call home, but as he stated to Wolf, this wasn't his home. What the hell did he look like shacking up with some guy he just met?

His mom would kick his ass if Jaycee did something as stupid as that.

"So you're saying I can't leave this place...ever?"

Wolf shrugged. "If I'm with you, then you can go wherever you want. But you are not going back home. It isn't safe."

Jaycee rubbed his hand over the back of his neck, wondering what he was going to do. Wolf was way too big to try to wrestle with, and being injured, Jaycee wasn't going to be that fast.

Shit and double shit.

For a moment Jaycee wondered if he was still unconscious, dreaming all of this. But even he didn't have the imagination it took to conjure something like this up. It had to be real. And that thought freaked him the hell out. "What are you?"

The man blinked at Jaycee, and then smiled, showing those damn fangs that were scaring the shit out of Jaycee. "I am a winged beast," Wolf answered as if proud of the fact.

Right. That didn't clear a damn thing up. "I'm going to take a wild stab here and say that means you aren't human."

Wolf shook his head.

Jaycee's thoughts began to tumble, splintering into a million pieces as he staggered slightly, walking back toward the bed. He wasn't sure if he just had this conversation a moment ago, but Jaycee wanted to be very clear on the subject before he flipped out.

There was nothing worse than flipping out on a misunderstanding, and Jaycee was very good at freaking the hell out and then thinking things through later. Yeah, he had always had an overactive imagination, but this was beyond anything he could have ever thought of.

A winged beast?

Crap.

"What exactly is a winged beast?"

"I am a vampire with wings…and a little something else thrown in for good measure," Wolf stated with a chuckle. Jaycee didn't get the joke.

He glanced around the room as if in a dream, and then his anger thundered through the room. His body was vibrating with anger and confusion. It confused him that Wolf was standing there telling him all of this like it was normal. It confused him that he had stumbled into some unknown world with hounds and winged vampires when all he had been trying to do was go home from work. And it really confused him the way Wolf kept looking at Jaycee like he was the jam to the man's jelly. He grabbed some small glass figurine from the side table and hurled it at Wolf. "Stay the fuck away from me!"

Overreaction kicking in big-time.

"Calm down, Jaycee." Wolf held his hands up in front of him in a nonthreatening manner. Jaycee wasn't falling for it. The man had just claimed to be some weird freaking vampire and even had fangs!

"Don't use my damn name. You could be trying to put a damn hex on me or something," he replied furiously.

Wolf twisted his lips to the side, giving him a look as if Jaycee was daft. "I'm a winged beast, not a voodoo priest."

"Same difference," Jaycee snarled as he backed away, looking for something else to toss at the man. He jumped up onto the bed, scooting quickly across it as he kept his eyes on Wolf. He hated arguing, fighting even more, but he was scared. He didn't know where he was or what was going on around him. Wolf wasn't human, and Jaycee was terrified the man was going to try something evil. He didn't know what a winged beast was, and Wolf could be blowing smoke up his ass when he said he wasn't going to hurt Jaycee. How did he know Wolf was telling the truth? He didn't. "If you try and eat me, I'll kick your ass."

Wolf crossed his arms over his chest, giving Jaycee a look that said *yeah right*. That look pissed Jaycee off even further. He may be human, and unable to fight Wolf, but fuck if he was lying down and taking whatever Wolf had in mind. He had only one arm to hurl the objects, but Jaycee was going to try his best to clobber the man in the head. That was the only way he was going to make it out of this room.

"You're being ridiculous."

"Fuck you," Jaycee said angrily as he got to his feet on the opposite side of the bed. "Put yourself in my shoes."

"I am not going to hurt you."

Jaycee froze, blinking his eyes a few times and staring directly at Wolf's mouth. He knew for damn sure that Wolf's lips hadn't moved. "Did–Did you just talk to me in my head?" He swallowed hard, wondering if he hadn't stepped into a real nightmare. If he had, at least the nightmare held a very hot guy.

Shit, he needed to stop thinking like that. The guy wasn't human and all Jaycee could do was check the man's package out. He needed his head examined. Wolf may be the first man to show Jaycee some attention, but it was attention he was pretty sure he didn't want. Jaycee just couldn't understand why the first guy to notice him in a heated way hadn't been human. His luck hadn't been all that great, but Jaycee didn't think it was that bad.

"I'm going to ignore the whole talking in my head thing," Jaycee said as he glanced around, spotting a book lying on a small table. He grabbed it, hefting it toward Wolf, who dodged it easily. "I'm going to ignore it because I'm going insane. You did *not* just talk to me in my head. I just imagined that."

"If it makes you sleep better at night," Wolf said as he stood there, his big beefy arms crossed over a very broad chest.

"What would make me sleep better at night is going home and being in my own bed. Will you let me go?" Jaycee asked, although he already knew that answer.

"No," Wolf replied as he shook his head. "The hound that came after you may be dead, but rest assured, the others know about you now."

"Others?" There were more of those things? Just facing one had made Jaycee want to piss himself, and there were more? Maybe Wolf's offer wasn't so bad. Jaycee paused in his search for missiles as he thought about another one of those things coming after him. "What about my roommates? Are they safe?"

"It was you who was marked, not them," Wolf said as he sat on the side of the bed, resting his arms on his thick thighs. Damn if the man didn't look good against the white spread. Jaycee wanted to see what Wolf—No, he didn't. He had to stop lusting after this lunatic. He forced himself to concentrate on the conversation, ignoring his horny cock.

"Marked? Please stop feeding me tidbits of what is going on and give it to me all at once."

Wolf's emerald-green eyes looked wary. It might be the whole throwing things at the man, or it could be that fact that Jaycee was freaking the hell out. But Jaycee didn't care. He wanted answers. He knew he overreacted first and then thought things through later, but anyone would lose their minds if they went from their ordinary lives to this in a span of just a few hours. No one could blame him for overreacting.

Wolf rubbed his hand over his chin, eyeing Jaycee warily. "I'm not sure you can handle what I have to say. You seem perfectly happy throwing things at me instead of calmly sitting down and listening."

Jaycee felt the heat rush to his face, but wasn't going to apologize for his behavior. It was the only thing perfectly normal around here. "I would say sorry, but you have to admit, the things you are telling me aren't something a human hears every day.

Great, now *he* was using the word *human*. Jaycee watched as a smile spread across Wolf's face. The smile filled his face, giving it personality and charm. He knew Wolf was a good-looking man, but his smile seemed to amplify his green eyes and fantastic mouth. A mouth that would look good wrapped around his—*Stop it!*

The man was smiling as if he knew Jaycee was lusting after him. There was no way the man could know, but hell if Wolf's eyes weren't glimmering with the knowledge. He cleared his throat and the heat left his eyes, replaced by a touch of anger. "When a hound goes after someone on purpose, that person is marked. There is nothing anyone can do to stop a hound but kill him."

"But you just said the one that came after me is dead," Jaycee pointed out. "So it should be safe for me now, right?"

Wolf slowly shook his head. Jaycee had a bad feeling about what the guy was about to say. "There are other hounds. They will take up the hell dweller's task. Theo was marked, but the hell dwellers after him are still alive. We fight to keep Theo alive. Now we will fight to keep you alive."

Gee, just like that. No big deal. Wolf said it as if it was an everyday occurrence.

Jaycee wanted to ask who the hell Theo was. It bothered him that he felt a pang of jealously at the mention of another man's name coming from Wolf. He didn't know Wolf. Why should Jaycee care who Theo was?

"So until all the hell dwellers are dead, I'm screwed?"

The next smile Wolf gave him was sad. It softened his features, but didn't make Jaycee feel at ease. "I'm afraid that killing all of the dwellers is an impossible task, *zaterio*. There are as many dwellers as there are humans, if not more."

Shit.

"How? If there were that many, wouldn't we know about them?"

"Hell is a very large place. It is filled with dwellers. They have always dwelled in hell, until recently. Many have been freed by a madman named Boromyr. We cannot put the hounds back once they are free, so we must kill them."

Jaycee took a seat on the side of the bed. He forgot about his fit and took in everything Wolf was telling him. It was too much. It was impossible, but hell if Jaycee didn't believe every word. He had seen things that were impossible in the past few hours. He didn't want to believe that the things going on could be true, but he wasn't going to stick his head in the sand and pretend they weren't. "So, in other words, I'm stuck here because they will keep coming after me until I'm dead?"

"Exactly."

"But," Jaycee began, shaking his head, trying to understand it all, "why me?"

"That I do not know. I'm guessing that they knew you were my *zaterio*. Although I haven't a clue how they would know."

Jaycee furrowed his brows at the word Wolf kept using. He knew it was some sort of endearment from the way the guy was using it, but he didn't know what it meant. "What is a *zaterio*?"

Wolf's eyes gleamed with something Jaycee couldn't decipher. The green seemed to lighten as he smiled at Jaycee. For a second in time, Jaycee became lost in that smile. It was as if the moon and the stars themselves had come down and were sparkling right in front of him. Jaycee shook his head, chasing away those ridiculous thoughts. Granted, it was a stunning look, but Jaycee shouldn't be comforted by it.

He should be trying to get the hell out of here.

Wolf tilted his head, giving Jaycee a boyish look with a touch of that smile lingering. "It means that you are my mate. You are to spend the rest of eternity at my side, Jaycee."

"Says who?" Jaycee squeaked as he jumped up from the bed, his head spinning at what Wolf had just told him. "You may be hot, but you're still a damn stranger, a nonhuman stranger."

"That can be remedied," Wolf said as he stood, walking around the bed, quickly closing the gap between them.

"Back off!" Jaycee warned as his back hit the wall. He ground his back teeth when pain shot down his injured arm. Damn, that hurt. "Don't even think about it."

"Don't think about what, Jaycee?" Wolf asked, but his eyes told Jaycee that the man knew exactly what Jaycee was referring to. It was a heated look that told Jaycee that Wolf wanted many hours of pleasure from him.

Jaycee stared at Wolf, feeling tightness in his groin. He didn't understand what was going on, but he didn't like it. He didn't even know Wolf. His body argued that that wasn't important, but Jaycee knew that it was. He wanted to have some sort of emotional attachment to a guy before jumping into bed. Jaycee had always felt that way, even if no one had given him the time of day yet. He knew he couldn't just drop his pants and have at it. That wasn't him.

Jaycee just did not do casual sex.

His roommates had called him a prude, but he wasn't going to change who he was, not for them, and not for Wolf. No matter how sexy the man...er...thing...er...beast...was.

"About remedying a damn thing, Wolf," Jaycee finally answered. "Just back the hell off."

"I would not touch you against your will, Jaycee." The anger slipped back into Wolf's eyes. Jaycee could deal with anger better than lust. Anger was something he was familiar with. Lust was something that was baffling him. It was scaring him more than the things after him. Jaycee wasn't sure how to handle the emotions rushing through him right now. They felt wonderful and terrifying at the same time. His cock was rock hard, and his heart was beating out of control. But the predominant feeling was fear.

Wolf was a very big man.

Wolf tilted his head back and gave one good sniff to the air, his eyes darting to Jaycee, and Jaycee watched as the heat left Wolf's eyes as he took a step back. "Are you hungry?" Wolf asked, throwing Jaycee way off with the quick change in subject. He hadn't been expecting that question.

"A little," he replied nervously. "But you just admitted that you were a vampire. Doesn't that mean you drink blood and hang upside down in a cave when you sleep?"

"Where in the hell did you hear that one?" Wolf asked.

"What, the drinking blood?"

"No, the hanging upside down part."

"So you *do* drink blood?"

Wolf gave him a hesitant glance and then sighed. "I am a vampire, Jaycee. I drink blood to sustain my life, but I also eat food. We have a very well-stocked kitchen. Come on, let's go eat."

"Okay, but if we end up in some sort of feeding room, I'm staking you through the heart, buddy." Jaycee walked around the side of the bed, hurrying toward the door.

"The only feeding room you are going to is the kitchen. Although, some of the men eat as if they are in front of a trough." Wolf chuckled as he followed behind Jaycee.

Jaycee had a feeling Wolf was staring at his ass as he walked out of the bedroom.

Chapter Three

Wolf was so damn pumped that his mate made it through the attack that he wanted to do a little happy dance. His *zaterio* was safe, awake, and ornery as hell.

Gods, he was in love.

He understood that his mate was scared. But what confused him was the scent of fear on Jaycee when Wolf had gotten closer. All he had wanted was a kiss. The negative emotion coming off of his *zaterio* had confused Wolf. Why would Jaycee fear a kiss?

"Hey, Wolf, who do we have here?" Nikoli, one of the winged beasts, asked as he walked down the hallway, taking a drink from a glass filled with what looked to be ice tea. Wolf's eyes snapped to his mate, watching Jaycee run his hands over one of the bedroom doors. The wood was ornately carved with symbols, spells their leader, Nazaryth, had placed on the mountain to keep anyone from finding them and to keep them safe.

Jaycee abandoned the bedroom door he was currently inspecting to glance at the next one. Wolf shook his head. The mating heat was making his skin feel tight, itchy, and he could feel his hands clenching and unclenching to grab Jaycee and run back to his bedroom. His groin felt like a hot rod was branding him as he gazed at his mate innocently running his lithe, long fingers over the carved wood, and wished to the gods it was his cock that Jaycee was brushing his fingertips over.

Since Jaycee had woken up, Wolf's cock had stayed hard. It was painful as hell. He wanted relief so badly that he had to fight not to reach out for his mate. The longer his cock remained unserviced, the

bitchier Wolf felt. He had also noticed that as the hours ticked by, the lust was only growing stronger inside of him. No wonder a winged beast went mad. Wolf wasn't sure he would last two whole days.

"According to Wolf, I'm his Cheerio. But my mom calls me Jaycee," his mate said as he turned toward Nikoli with a tight grin on his face. "And according to Wolf, I'm stuck here until the bad little doggies are no longer interested in me—which, according to Wolf, is when hell freezes over. So, who are you?"

Wolf could see Nikoli fighting the smile that was pulling at his lips, and then the man started laughing. "Oh, this is going to be fun."

"He is Nikoli," Wolf answered his *zaterio*.

"Is he a vampire as well?" Jaycee asked as he began to walk down the hallway, studying the next door. Wolf was curious as to why Jaycee was so damn interested in the wooden doors when all he could think about was sinking his cock deep into his mate's ass. Didn't Jaycee feel the attraction? Didn't he want to get sweaty in the sheets as they knocked boots? Good god, he needed to stop hanging with Silo. The computer geek was corrupting his damn mind.

"No," Nikoli replied. "I'm a winged beast."

"Same difference." Jaycee waved Nikoli off. "Semantics."

"Haven't claimed him yet, have you?" Nikoli looked from Wolf's obvious erection and then to his face, a sparkle of humor in his dark eyes. "Poor bastard."

"I can hear you two," Jaycee sang as he moved further down the hallway. "I'm human, not dumb."

"Same difference," Nikoli teased. "Semantics."

"Take that back!" Wolf gave a deadly growl as he grabbed Nikoli by the front of his shirt, twisting the fabric in his hand as he shoved the beast into the wall. "Apologize to my *zaterio* for the disrespect you've just shown him."

"It's cool. I was just bantering with him. I meant no harm, Wolf." Nikoli held his hands up in a surrender gesture as he glanced from Wolf to Jaycee. "We cool, little man?"

"Just as long as you never in your life call me little man again, we're cool." Jaycee patted Wolf's hand. "You can let him go now."

When Jaycee's hand touched Wolf's, his entire body stiffened and a warm flow of desire spread throughout his body. He wanted the man. Wolf felt hot and bothered, multiplied by one hundred, and the need to claim his mate was overwhelming. He gritted his teeth as he closed his eyes, breathing out slowly through his mouth.

His *zaterio* was also too damn close to Nikoli, Wolf realized when he opened his eyes. Wolf's chest vibrated as he released Nikoli and pulled Jaycee into his arms, turning so his mate wasn't standing right there in front of the beast.

"Now what?" Jaycee asked as he glanced up at Wolf, who was letting out a low and rumbling growl. Gods, Wolf just couldn't think straight with Jaycee in his arms. He could only think of Jaycee writhing under him as he fucked the man senseless. His wings fluttered furiously as sweat began to surface all over his body. His cock was pulsing, throbbing, aching to be released and to find release. Wolf's entire body was tingling and buzzing with need.

"Now I get the hell away from you before Wolf tries to pull my tongue out through my ass," Nikoli said as he walked toward the living room.

"That sounds painful," Jaycee said from behind Wolf.

Wolf closed his eyes for a moment and prayed for strength. Jaycee's scent was so strong that it was clouding his mind and pushing his reasoning away. His beast was getting closer to the surface at the same time. Wolf wanted nothing more than to take his mate right here in the hallway and bind them together for all eternity. It was something all winged beasts craved, to find their mates and claim them, but having his *zaterio* so close, and unclaimed, was playing havoc with Wolf's mind and body.

He needed a moment away from his mate. Wolf wasn't sure he could hold his composure much longer. His body was coiled and ready, and Jaycee wasn't. "I'll take you to the kitchen now."

Jaycee walked around Wolf, his fingers sliding sensually over Wolf's bare arm. Wolf shuddered and pulled his arm away.

"Zaterio, you are killing me here."

Jaycee stilled, glancing up at Wolf, and then began to point his finger between his head and Wolf's. "You're doing that mind thingy again."

And Jaycee was making Wolf's cock so hard that he feared it would shatter into a thousand pieces in his pants. Taking a deep and unsteady breath, Wolf stepped back. "Kitchen."

Jaycee nodded, but kept his head tilted back as he stared at Wolf. "Kitchen," he repeated.

Even with the need slowly burning behind Jaycee's chocolate-brown eyes, Wolf wasn't going to take any chances with his mate. He wasn't going to rush him. Not that much anyway.

He did only have two days, after all.

But what Wolf discovered while tending to his wounded mate was that the mating heat was absent when his mate was injured. Fate may be a fickle little bitch, but at least it had a conscience.

But now that Jaycee was well, it was like the heat had gone into overdrive. He waved a hand toward the end of the hall and then began to walk stiffly, feeling his hard cock pulsing in his pants with every step.

Jaycee yelped as Wolf growled when the very castle itself rocked on its foundation.

"What was that?" Jaycee asked as he grabbed Wolf's arm. "Was that an earthquake?"

It wasn't an earthquake. Wolf had an idea what it was as he grabbed his mate's hand and rushed toward the monitors that sat on one wall in the living room. The living room was in total chaos. The winged beasts were shouting and running toward the same wall as Wolf.

"What happened?" Vydeck shouted as Nazaryth scanned the monitors.

"Are all these men vampires?" Jaycee whispered from behind Wolf.

"They are all winged beasts, except Theo."

"Good to know," Jaycee replied as Wolf watched his commander, waiting for Nazaryth to tell them what had just happened.

"Hell hounds?" Dog asked.

"No," Nazaryth said as he shook his head, his face grim. "I believe our *gift* has finally arrived."

Wolf's stomach knotted at the reminder of the gift King Zephyr sent every one hundred years. They all had thought the king had forgotten since their anniversary of being banished had come and gone.

But they weren't so lucky.

"What did he send?" Ruthless asked.

Nazaryth slowly turned from the monitors, his face slightly pale. Wolf was not going to like this. It took something colossal to make Nazaryth look that way. There was very little the commander feared, and what he did fear made angels wet themselves.

"Two very large brimstone demons."

Wolf hurried over to the monitors and saw the ten-foot creatures slamming their oversized fists into the side of the hangar. They had two large black horns on either side of their heads that curled crudely under each ear. They also had one small black horn that jutted from their chins. They were pasty white, as if they had never seen a day in the sun in their miserable lives.

Their foreheads slanted downward, and thick, black claws extended from their fingers. Wolf knew that their claws were deadly to *any* being that came into contact with them.

But the nastiest part about the demons was the fact that they could spit acid. A winged beast could survive the acid spit, but they would scar. It was one of the very few things that *could* scar them.

King Zephyr must really miss the winged beasts to send such a special *gift*.

"What in the hell are those?" Jaycee asked, his voice barely a whisper.

"Brimstone demons," Wolf answered.

"Yeah, I heard the first guy. But what are they?"

"Very nasty creatures who have an IQ of a shoestring, but are damn strong," Dog answered for Wolf and then turned to Nazaryth. "So what's the plan, boss?"

Nazaryth ran his hand over the back of his neck, staring intently at the monitors as he shook his head. "We shift into our beast forms and fight. We can't allow them to reach civilization. They would tear through Zeus's town like a hot knife through butter."

The winged beasts began to shift, but Wolf pulled his *zaterio* over by Nazaryth's mate, Theo. "Can you watch Jaycee?"

"You got it. I think this time I'll pass on the fighting," Theo said as he looked over at the monitors. "Those aren't hounds, and I'm only a wolf shifter. You can go play peek-a-boo without me."

"Wolf shifter?" Jaycee asked as he swallowed, eyeing Theo like he was one of the demons.

Wolf cupped Jaycee's face, planting a quick kiss on his mate's nose. Anywhere else and Wolf wasn't going to make it out of the castle to fight. The mating heat was still riding him strong. "I'll answer any questions you have when I return. Stay by Theo. He has half a chance of protecting you if things go wrong."

"Go wrong?" Jaycee asked, his eyes as wide as twin moons.

"Thanks for the vote of confidence," Theo snapped. "I'll go sit in a corner in my wolf form and lick my balls while you *men* go out and fight."

Wolf was not trying to get into a debate with Nazaryth's mate. Theo had a way with words, and Wolf didn't have time to tongue spar with the man. "Thanks."

Wolf took one last long glance at his mate as he released his beast and headed for one of the exits. He prayed they defeated the demons,

because if they didn't, Jaycee had bigger things to worry about than hounds coming after him.

* * * *

Jaycee stared at the monitors and swore he was watching a movie instead. It had to be. There was no way he was really seeing this. There were two fucking demons, actual demons, on the monitors, beating the holy hell out of that hangar.

"This can't be real," he whispered.

"Oh, it's real," Theo commented from beside him. "But as long as we stay inside, the spells should protect us."

"Should?" Jaycee asked as he glanced at the man. "Should?" he said a little louder this time, his voice taking on a higher pitch. "*Should* doesn't sound so damn good right about now."

He was going to be sick. Jaycee couldn't get over the fact that he was seeing two demons right before his very eyes. "Where did they come from?"

"Hell," Theo answered. "And from their name, I would suspect the very bowels of hell."

Oh, no. Jaycee had to get the fuck out of there. Wolf was gorgeous and all, but not even a good-looking man who wanted him was going to convince Jaycee to stick around this place.

"Where do you think you're going?" Theo asked as Jaycee headed toward the hallway he had just come down.

"Bathroom," he called over his shoulder, wondering how in the hell he could get out of this crazy-ass place. There had to be a way out. All places had exits, even castles. He could feel the panic take hold and pull him along quickly. Those were demons on the monitors, hounds were after him, and Theo was some kind of wolf. He felt like he was going to be sick. As much as he wanted to stop and think this through rationally, Jaycee didn't see anything rational about this whole bizarre situation.

No, running would be very good right now.

"Don't be too long." Theo's voice drifted toward Jaycee, but he was running by the time he had heard it. First he was attacked by hounds from hell. Then Jaycee was rescued by a freaking vampire with wings—and the wings were still debatable since he hadn't seen them yet—and now there were two brimstone demons knocking at the door? Wolf must be out of his ever-loving mind if he thought Jaycee was going to stick around for the next show to begin.

This place was a psychotic loony bin from…well, hell.

Jaycee began to search every room in the long hallway, but couldn't find a way out of this place. He knew Theo would probably come looking for him soon, so he was running out of time.

How in the hell had the vampires with invisible wings gotten out? He would rather take his chances with the doggies from hell than those two extremely large creatures trying to get in. Jaycee didn't care if they were dumber than doorknobs. They had claws and horns. That was good enough for him.

But as he searched every room, unable to find an exit, Jaycee was beginning to think he would never get out of here. Where in the hell were the doors?

He slid out of the last room he had searched, inching his way down the hallway. Jaycee stuck his head around the corner, scanning the living room, and saw that it was empty. Theo must be searching for him.

Let the man search. Jaycee was going to keep looking for a way out until someone stopped him. He shot across the living room and headed down the hallway on the opposite side of the room. Jaycee's heart rate picked up when he saw a large wooden door.

He crossed his fingers and then pushed it open. There were steps leading downward, small torches to light the way. He prayed he didn't run into anything from hell down below as he glanced over his shoulder to make sure the wolf shifter—gods, he couldn't believe he was thinking that—hadn't come back.

Jaycee blew out a long breath and then stepped into the tunnel. When he reached the bottom, he saw he was in a room full of plants. They were everywhere. He wasn't sure where he was, but Jaycee searched quickly for a door.

His heart beat faster as he saw a large metal door on the other end of the room. He wasn't sure where the door led, but it was better than going back upstairs.

He just hoped like hell that it didn't lead right into the battle outside.

* * * *

"Watch the acid!" Ruthless shouted as Wolf flew out of the way just in time. The spit missile had barely missed his head. It smelled like sulfur and gasoline, with a side of vomit. Wolf was ready to upchuck his last meal as the smell lingered behind.

"Stab their fucking marks!" Nazaryth shouted as he flew over one of the demon's heads, grabbing the sword from the sheath down his spine and pulling it free, slicing the sword through the air, missing by a hair's breadth.

The damn things were quick to be so lumbering.

Every creature that came from hell had a mark somewhere on their heads, just like the hell hounds. They could be killed and sent back to hell. The trick was stabbing them in their mark. The demons may be dimwitted, but they knew to keep their mark protected.

They had chased the demons to the other side of the mountain, the side where no humans should see them accidently from the road. Although they lived far enough back, it would be just their luck to have a lost human stumble upon them. Wolf was relieved they had moved. He didn't want one of those vile things to get inside the castle. There were spells and wards to protect the castle, but even dimwitted demons had dumb luck, as Nazaryth would say.

Plus they were in their beast form.

Try and explain that to a human.

Trap and Silo flew around the demons' heads, trying their best to confuse the beast as Renato went in for the kill. But as soon as Renato got close enough, the demon spit. Renato shouted and flew past Nazaryth, holding his arm with his hand.

Damn. This was getting ugly.

"Be careful, damn it!" Nazaryth shouted. "I don't need any of you dying on me."

Wolf hadn't planned on dying. He sure as shit hoped that wasn't his fate. He swung around the demon that had just spit at Renato and jabbed his sword toward the damn thing's head, but the demon moved out of the way in the nick of time.

It felt like one big-ass game of cat and mouse. It seemed no matter what strategy they used, the demons were on alert, getting out of the way of the blade in time.

"What the—"

"They vanished!" Layne shouted. "Where in the fuck did they go?"

Nazaryth growled as he flew toward the top of the mountain. "Wherever they went, you better believe they'll be back."

Wolf glanced toward the west and wondered if the demons were going into a populated area, but Nazaryth didn't seem concerned. The commander must know something, or he would be giving the command to chase after them.

He forgot about the demons as the mating heat kicked in big-time. Wolf dropped down onto one knee as he landed and then walked toward the entrance to his bedroom. That was what he loved about this castle so much. Each room had a secret passageway to the outside. No beast could ever become trapped. There was even one off of the living room, and an exit down in the room they housed the healing plants in.

He waved his hand in front of a large boulder, watching as it slid aside. Wolf slowly returned to his human form as he entered his bedroom. He smiled over at the bed, his mind wandering to the wicked sex he and his *zaterio* were sure to have real soon. Jaycee was sexy, witty, comical, and someone Wolf couldn't wait to have in his bed.

He had heard about the mating ritual from Nazaryth, how special it was, how intimate it would be. The commander had said that it was something a winged beast could only experience with their *zaterio*.

Wolf couldn't wait.

He sauntered into the living room to find Theo over by the monitors playing kissy-face with Nazaryth, but Wolf didn't see Jaycee. He ignored the mated pair as he walked into the kitchen, feeling his cock harden and his skin grow tight as he rolled his shoulders, hearing his vertebrae crack from the tension.

Wolf stilled when he didn't see his mate in the kitchen either.

Where could Jaycee be?

"Theo," Wolf called out as he turned on his heel.

"What?" Theo asked, breaking apart from Nazaryth.

"Where is Jaycee?" Theo chewed the side of his lip and Wolf's heart plummeted. "Where is my *zaterio*?"

"He said he had to use the bathroom."

Wolf cocked his head, his eyes burning into Theo's amber ones. "And?"

Theo tossed his hands up, shaking his head back and forth. "And when he took too long, I went searching for him."

Wolf growled. He did not like the fact that he had to drag the information out of Theo. If the shifter wasn't the commander's mate, he would throttle the guy. "Please tell me there is more?"

"And," Theo said as he glanced from Nazaryth to Wolf, "I couldn't find him."

Wolf threw back his head and roared, his beast reemerging as he stormed down the hallway. *"Zaterio, where are you?"*

Wolf waited, but his mate didn't reply.

He took the exit in his bedroom and flew out into the night, going on the hunt for his mate.

Chapter Four

Jaycee sat very still in the passenger seat, knowing that hitchhiking was a stupid move. But if he hadn't taken a ride from the stranger, then he would still be walking back to Pride Pack Valley. He probably would have gotten caught by either a hound or Wolf, too.

Neither was an acceptable option to him.

"Where you coming from?" the stranger asked from beside him.

"Hell," Jaycee answered, gazing out the window and missing Wolf for some strange reason. The man wasn't human. Jaycee should not be missing him. So why did his damn chest hurt so much? Just thinking about Wolf's face made Jaycee feel a pang of remorse for what he had just done. Maybe he should have left a note explaining why he had run. Would Wolf worry about him? The man was at his bedside when Jaycee was unconscious. Maybe the winged vampire really did care.

But how? They didn't even know each other. Jaycee wrung his hands in his lap, wishing that the feeling of leaving the best part of his life behind would go away. It didn't make any damn sense to him.

"That bad?" the man asked, pulling Jaycee from his thoughts.

"Yeah." Jaycee didn't want to talk right now. He wanted to get as far away from this place as he could. He would get to his house and then figure out what to do from there. It wasn't like he could drive his own car. It was still parked three blocks from his house and not running.

"Just keep telling yourself that things will get better, son. You left. That's the important thing."

Jaycee sighed. If only it were that easy. He may have left, but he had a feeling he wouldn't be safe until he left town. And maybe not even then. He wished he could talk to someone about what was going on, but the man sitting next to him would probably have Jaycee locked up if he started telling the guy that there were more than just humans on earth. There was no one he could talk to, and that thought depressed him.

"Make a right up here." Jaycee pointed.

"I run a ranch for people needing help. You can come stay there if you'd like."

No way was Jaycee going any further than he had to with this guy. Who offered to take a stray in? The man must be psycho or something. "No, thanks. You can just drop me off at home."

The guy nodded. Jaycee had been skeptical to take a ride in the first place. The man was freaking huge! But he weighed his options and picked the lesser of two evils. Or was that three?

"My name's Pa Lakeland. If you ever need a place to stay, go talk to Zeus and he'll guide you to me."

The mayor? "Uh, okay."

Pa Lakeland pulled into Jaycee's driveway and let him out. He waved to the man and hurried inside, but not before checking all around him for the nasty little doggies. He wasn't going to get caught off guard again.

Jaycee hurried inside and packed a bag, grabbing everything he could carry and then stopped when he saw Rico sitting on the couch, the television going as the man sat there texting.

"Hey, Rico, can I borrow your car?"

"Go ahead," Rico said, never looking up from his phone. Jaycee was tempted to tell Rico that he was running as far away as he could, but he knew Rico wouldn't care. Rico was the type that just floated through life, acting as if nothing ever bothered him. Jaycee didn't get the guy. He collected insurance money once a month for his dad's death, so Rico assumed that meant he didn't have to work or do anything with his life.

Jaycee shook his head. It was such a waste of a good person. He grabbed the keys by the door and hurried to the tree lawn where Rico parked by the curb. He tossed the bag into the back and then pulled away.

Hopefully he could get as far away from this place before anyone figured out where he was. Wolf finding out wouldn't be so bad, Jaycee decided, but the doggies finding out was very bad.

* * * *

Jaycee drove down the road, continuously checking his rearview mirror. All he saw was the pitch-black countryside behind him. He had been driving for hours, and his eyes were beginning to burn. He had no clue where he was going, but any place other than Pride Pack Valley was good enough for him.

Alaska sounded good right about now.

Jaycee rubbed his sternum as he drove, feeling a deep sense of loss. The feeling of remorse was deepening the further away he drove. He still wasn't sure why he was feeling this way. He had lived in Pride Pack Valley his entire life and the only person he should be missing was his mom.

And he knew he was denying who he was really missing. But how? He had just met Wolf. How could he miss him so much that his chest actually hurt? He couldn't understand it, but there was a weight sitting in his chest when he thought about Wolf.

Jaycee was nuts to think that way. Wolf was a vampire with wings who fought doggies from hell, and big, ugly things with horns and really sharp-looking claws. Jaycee would be nuts to stick around.

So why did he want to turn around?

"Zaterio, where are you? Talk to me, please."

And that was another thing. How in the hell could someone talk inside his head? There was no way Jaycee was answering voices in his head. He brushed a falling tear away from his eye with the palm of his hand as he kept on driving. But the longer he drove, the harder it became not to turn around and run back to the beast.

He needed to get out of that crazy town, find somewhere safe, somewhere that didn't have things from hell, or vampires, or even men who shifted into animals. He needed someplace to lay low.

Jaycee saw a large white sign ahead that read *Welcome to Brac Village*. That sounded like a nice place to hide. It was a few hours from Pride Pack Valley. Jaycee was pretty sure they didn't have any problems with strange creatures and men who could change into weird things.

"Zaterio, you are in danger. You must answer me."

Yeah, so not happening. Jaycee really did want to let Wolf know he was all right. The man had saved his life, after all. But he was afraid that if he spoke to Wolf, the vampire would have some sort of mental GPS and lock onto Jaycee's location.

He couldn't chance it.

The only place Jaycee spotted to sleep was a bed-and-breakfast, and all of the lights were out in the house. He wasn't sure if he was allowed to wake anyone to rent a room. It wasn't a motel, so he didn't know the proper protocol.

He decided to park his borrowed car in front of Tate's Resource Center and then killed the motor, balling up in the driver's seat. All he needed was a few hours of sleep. If he could just get a few hours of sleep, he would be able to think more clearly and then figure out what he was going to do from there.

His LED watch said that it was three in the morning. Jaycee had left work at three in the afternoon, and his life had turned to total chaos since then. He may have gotten to sleep a few hours after his attack, but Jaycee felt drained. All the excitement had zapped any energy that Jaycee had.

"Hey, you all right in there?"

Jaycee turned his head to see a very tall and muscular man standing by the driver's window, staring right down at him. He froze. The guy was pretty damn big. As Jaycee slowly lifted his eyes, he was staring right into the man's...silver eyes? Were they really silver?

"I'm Remi. Do you need a place to stay for the night?"

Jaycee wasn't sure if he should answer the man. The tall blond scared the shit out of him. The guy had an easy smile on his face and squatted down so that they were eye level, but that didn't help the knot in his stomach.

"I'm not trying to scare you. I help out at the resource center at night just in case anyone parks their car in front of it and needs help." The man winked at Jaycee and then pointed over to the building behind him. "But if you prefer, I can call Taylor Tate, the guy who runs this place."

Jaycee nodded. "Please." Because he was not getting out of the car with this big muscle-bound dude standing right there. *So not happening.* He didn't just run from strange creatures to get murdered by some large human.

"It's fine," Remi said. "If you feel safer waiting in your car, then do so. I won't let whoever is after you bother you again."

Jaycee was quite certain that Remi couldn't take on Wolf. He appreciated the offer though. The guy had no idea what Jaycee was running from. He bet Remi wouldn't be offering shelter if he knew.

Jaycee sat up when Remi began to talk into his phone, wondering if the guy was really calling the man who ran the resource center, or calling in his buddies to come have a good time with him.

Please let the guy be on the up-and-up.

"Who, zaterio? Who is bothering you? Please talk to me."

Damn, he hadn't meant to talk to Wolf inside his head. It was just a thought, not a conversation he wanted to have. Jaycee bit his lip, glancing at Remi and wondering if he should tell Wolf where he was.

Jaycee decided to wait and see what happened. If the man was setting him up, then he would call for help. It would be a last resort, though. Jaycee nearly jumped out of skin when Remi knocked on the window with his knuckles.

"What?"

"Taylor is on his way. He should be here in a few minutes."

"Thank you." Jaycee rolled his eyes as he glanced away. He was probably being polite to a serial killer or something. Gods, he was so tired. He was starting to sound crazy even in his own head.

Jaycee kept a close eye on Remi as he waited for this Taylor guy to show up. His eyes started to droop a couple of times, and he found himself making them as wide as possible to stay awake. He probably looked like a complete goober, but at that point, he just didn't care. He wanted a safe place where he could sleep for several hours, and then a good meal, and then he was getting the fuck out of wherever he was.

After what seemed like hours but was probably only a few minutes, a truck pulled into the space beside Jaycee and a man climbed out. He walked over and talked to Remi for a moment, both men gesturing toward Jaycee.

Jaycee blew out a sigh of relief when Remi nodded and walked away. That guy was scary big. The man who had gotten out of the truck walked closer and then leaned his hip against the front fender of Jaycee's car, just waiting. Jaycee glanced around to make sure that Remi was gone and then slowly climbed from the vehicle.

"Hi, I'm Taylor Tate," the man said as he held out his hand. "I run this place."

"Jaycee."

"Why don't you come inside and we can talk, Jaycee?" Taylor gestured toward the building with his head. "You'll be safe in there. I promise."

Yeah, Jaycee wasn't taking Taylor's word for it, and he could see that Taylor knew that by the glint in his eyes. Taylor nodded and turned, walking toward the building. Jaycee stayed several steps behind him just in case he needed to run. He felt better when Taylor left the front door open and walked inside, moving to the opposite side of the room from Jaycee and his escape route.

"My job here is to make sure that people are safe," Taylor began as he sat down on the edge of a desk. "I met someone once who was in a lot of trouble. He had nowhere that he could go and no one to help him get out of the horrible situation he was in. After meeting him, I wanted to make sure that no one else was ever in that same position, not if there was some way that I could help."

"Did he get out?" Jaycee asked curiously.

"Yes." Taylor smiled. "He was actually the first man to take up a cot here. The building still pretty much had wet paint on the walls when he arrived."

"But he's safe, right?"

"He is. Thank you for asking. He found someone he truly cares about and he's happy."

Jaycee wished he knew he had the same outcome coming, but he knew he'd be crazy to think that. Taylor's first client may have had his happy ending, but Jaycee was pretty sure he was going to end up ripped to shreds by hell dwellers or forever pursued by winged vampires.

He was so screwed.

"I'd like to help you, Jaycee."

Jaycee snorted. "I'm not sure you can help me." He was pretty sure no one could help him. There didn't seem to be any protection against hell dwellers, demons, and whatever else was out there. And Jaycee didn't even want to think about that.

"I can listen if you want to talk."

Oh hell no! If he talked, he'd end up in a padded room for sure. Jaycee shook his head. "I don't think so."

"That's fine," Taylor replied. "You don't have to talk if you don't want to. But I am here in case you do, and whatever is said between us stays between us."

Jaycee nodded but he wasn't going to spill the beans. Seriously, he just—"There's this guy, and he thinks I belong to him." Jaycee inwardly groaned. It seemed his brain was dying to make sense of the situation. He just hoped Taylor didn't have him committed.

"Did he do that to your arm?" Taylor asked as he pointed to the white gauze wrapped around Jaycee's arm.

Jaycee glanced down at his arm, surprised that he had forgotten the wound. "No, he didn't do this, but someone he knows did."

"Did he or anyone else hurt you in any other way?"

"No, but…" Jaycee shook his head. "They're scary, man, I mean fucking scary. I had to sneak away just to escape them. He said I could never leave and that I was—" *Nope, not going there.* Jaycee glanced at Taylor. "I just had to leave."

"I understand." Taylor waved his hands around the room. "You're welcome to stay here as long as you like. We don't have any other people in the center at the moment, so it's all yours."

"Thank you. I just need a place to sleep for a little while. It feels like I haven't slept in days."

"Take as long as you like." Taylor pushed away from the desk and started walking toward a hallway. "Come on, I'll show you where the dorm is. You can pretty much take any bed you want. There's also a shower facility if you want to get cleaned up."

"I just want to sleep for right now, but maybe I'll take you up on that shower in the morning."

Gods, he was so tired.

"Zaterio? Please answer me. You're in so much danger. I just want to make sure that you are safe."

"Fuck!" Jaycee pressed his hands against his temples as Wolf's voice floated through his head. Why wouldn't the guy leave him the hell alone? He couldn't even think without Wolf butting into his head.

"Jaycee, what's wrong?"

"He won't leave me alone," Jaycee whispered as he pushed the heels of his hands into his head. "He just keeps talking to me over and over again."

"He…keeps talking to you?"

Jaycee's head snapped up as he realized what he had done. *Oh, perfect.* Now Taylor thought he had a screw loose. Maybe he did. He heard voices in his head, after all.

"Is he talking to you in your head, Jaycee?"

Jaycee nodded, knowing beyond a shadow of a doubt that it was probably the dumbest thing he could do. He just couldn't think of any other answer for his behavior.

Taylor's eyebrows shot up. "Right now?"

Jaycee felt his face flush at the inquisitive look in Taylor's eyes. "Sort of?"

"Do you hear other voices?"

"No, just Wolf's."

"His name is Wolf?"

Crap. Maybe he should duct-tape his mouth shut. He was digging a deeper and deeper hole for himself. Soon he would be on the other side of the planet if he didn't stop talking.

"How long have you been hearing him in your head, Jaycee?"

Jaycee glanced down at his watch. "Um, about twelve hours or so, give or take an hour. I was unconscious for a while so I'm not exactly sure of when it started, but it had to be sometime after I got off work." *And got attacked by hell hounds.*

Taylor looked thoughtful. He wasn't staring at Jaycee like he'd lost his mind—which was pretty damn odd considering what Jaycee was confessing to the man. If roles were reversed, Jaycee would be ordering Taylor a straitjacket right about now.

Taylor looked as if he were collecting his thoughts and then paced back and forth, his brows furrowed as he glanced at the floor and then back at Jaycee. "Have you ever heard of mates, Jaycee?" Taylor asked.

Jaycee's eyes grew wide as he started to backpedal. His heart was slamming in his chest, and his throat went bone-dry. There was no fucking way Taylor knew about mates unless—"You're one of them!" What in the hell had he gotten himself into? It seemed no matter where he went, he wasn't safe. Were these kinds of people everywhere? Was no place safe enough for Jaycee to run to and hide?

Had the whole damn country gone mad and Jaycee wasn't handed the memo?

"Easy, Jaycee," Taylor said as he turned, holding his hands up. "I don't know what you're talking about, but I'm not a bad guy. I'm not one of them, whoever *them* is."

The hell he isn't.

Jaycee wasn't sure where he could go to get away from the madness. Nothing seemed real to him anymore. He had seen horrors in the past twelve hours that would probably give most people a coronary. And everyone wanted him to calm down? That was not going to happen. Not after seeing hounds from hell. Hell, damn it. That place was supposed to be myth. It wasn't supposed to be real.

And those demons…

"Get away from me!"

Taylor took a step back, but didn't leave. His expression was concerned, like he was trying to talk a man down from a ledge. And Jaycee felt like he was on one right now. He was teetering between what he thought he knew and what was really all around him.

"I promised you that you were safe here, Jaycee, and I stand by that promise. I swear no one is going to hurt you. I just need you to calm down and talk to me."

Jaycee didn't know who to trust anymore. He was so damn bone-weary tired and sick of running. He was dead on his feet and knew that if he left this place, this town, he wouldn't make it far. Even knowing Taylor was some sort of freak like every other person he had run into in the last twelve hours, he couldn't keep his eyes open. He was probably about to ask the wrong question, but Jaycee's adrenaline rush was zapped out of him that quickly. His head began to throb violently as he glanced around the center.

"Can I just lie down right now?" He would worry about things after he had some sleep. His eyes were burning, and he swayed slightly.

"Of course." Taylor waved his hand toward the back of the building. "There are cots back there, and Remi is on guard. I promise you nothing will happen while you sleep."

Jaycee managed a snort. "I wouldn't be too sure. Winged beasts are pretty damn big."

Taylor's hand hung in midair as he gaped at Jaycee. "Did you just say winged beast?"

Jaycee was too tired to care about the man's shocked reaction. All he wanted to do was lie down. His arm was killing him, and his headache was getting worse. Maybe when he was bright-eyed and bushy-tailed he would be able to figure out what to do.

Taylor pulled his phone from his pocket, walking down the hallway. Jaycee followed.

"Maverick, we have a situation."

That was an understatement.

"I have a winged beast's mate here," he spoke quickly into the phone.

Jaycee spotted a row of cots and lay down on the first one he could reach. "You're not going to tell Wolf that I'm here, are you?" Jaycee asked as he yawned. He kicked his shoes off and laid his head on the pillow, wishing he had some pain relievers for his arm. It was killing him.

"No," Taylor answered, but didn't look too sure about his answer.

"Whoever you are talking to, warn him about the hounds after me and the brimstone demons."

Taylor lowered the phone, his mouth hanging wide open. His eyebrows were arched so high that Jaycee thought they were going to slide off of the man's face. "You've got to be shitting me."

"I wish I were," Jaycee said as he turned over and closed his eyes.

* * * *

"Did he just say brimstone demons?" Maverick asked in astonishment.

"Yeah," Taylor answered as he stared at Jaycee fast asleep on the cot, "he did."

"I have to call Nazaryth, Taylor," Maverick said gently but firmly. "I have a feeling Jaycee is running because he doesn't understand about mates, but I can't have demons and hounds here in Brac Village."

"You can't," Taylor quickly argued as he walked toward the front of the resource center, away from the exhausted man. "I promised him that he would be safe. You can't let this Wolf guy know where he is. It would go against everything I had this shelter built for."

"Calm down," Maverick said and then sighed. "I'll tell Nazaryth not to say a word to Wolf about where Jaycee is, but his mate must be worried sick about him."

That was true. But Taylor wasn't going to rat the guy out and hand him over to the man Jaycee was running from. He would never forgive himself if something bad happened to Jaycee. The guy trusted him.

Taylor leaned against the door, glancing outside and watching his mate, Dagon, talk quietly to Remi, a smile lighting up his face at whatever they were discussing. Gods, how he loved Dagon. Taylor knew that his mate would go absolutely crazy if Taylor came up missing. He walked out onto the sidewalk, looking over the sleeping town, and knew he couldn't allow demons and hounds to invade the small community.

"I don't know what to do," he confessed.

"Whatever happens, Jaycee's safety comes first. You know that, Taylor. But I can't have our pack threatened in the process." Maverick sighed. "We're going to have to protect them both. Let your mate and Remi know what's going on. They deserve to have a heads-up. I'll call you if shit goes south."

"Same here," Taylor said before hanging up.

"Is everything all right, *cachorro*?" Dagon asked as he leaned against his truck, holding his arms out. Taylor quickly walked over, sliding into his mate's arms and instantly feeling safe and loved.

"He's a winged beast's mate."

Remi whistled low. "What are you going to do?"

Taylor shrugged as he inhaled his mate's scent. "I'm caught between a rock and a hard place. I won't hand him over to the man he's running from, but I have a feeling he's only running because he's scared. On the other hand, how can I keep mates apart?"

"You do whatever is best for the guy," Dagon answered. "We'll take care of the rest."

Yeah, Taylor knew that. But he was afraid the price was going to be extremely high, if not for Jaycee, then for Taylor's family.

He just prayed it didn't come to that.

Chapter Five

"What do you mean you can't tell me where he is?" Wolf growled the words out as he paced the living room. "I have thirty-six hours left, Nazaryth. You would watch me go mad?"

Nazaryth leaned against the living room wall, crossing his arms over his shoulder, his expression grim. "I'm caught between a rock and a hard place, Wolf."

"The hell you are!" Wolf shouted, feeling his anger and his terror ride the air like a hot, invisible mist. It swirled all around him, threatening to choke him. He wanted his *zaterio*. He felt the loss so deeply that it was nearly crippling him. Jaycee was out there all alone. There was no telling what trouble he was in, and his commander was between a rock and a hard place? "I've done nothing wrong to Jaycee. I haven't harmed him in any way. He's just scared. Tell me where he is, Commander."

"Have you tried contacting him?"

Wolf ran a hand down his face, trying his best to gain some measure of control. Nazaryth would annihilate him if he throttled the man, but fuck if it wasn't tempting. "Yes, but he won't answer me."

"I could go with him. You know, to make sure…" Nikoli trailed off, but Wolf fully understood what the beast was referring to and he didn't like it.

"So I won't hurt my *zaterio*?" Wolf growled the words out. "You think that I would harm the only man made for me? You would sit there and accuse me of abusing my mate?"

"No." Nikoli shook his head. "That's not what I meant."

"Then what did you mean?" Wolf asked, feeling his fangs emerging as his claws grew. The mating heat, along with the fear eating away inside of Wolf, was making him aggressive as hell. And if his wings didn't stop fucking fluttering he was going to cut the damn things off!

"You want me to tell you where your mate is while you are this aggressive?" Nazaryth asked.

"It will only get worse the longer I am away from him," Wolf reminded the winged beasts' leader. "The longer Jaycee remains unclaimed, the madder I will become."

Even Wolf could hear the desperation in his voice. He wasn't going to force Jaycee to mate with him, but Wolf didn't want to lose himself to insanity and have to be killed. No winged beast survived the madness. Wolf could feel it slowly building inside of him like a ticking time bomb.

He breathed in through his nose and out through his mouth, trying his best to calm down. It had been twelve hours since he had found his mate. Even with Jaycee being wounded, the mating heat had banked its embers, but hadn't gone away. Why in the fuck had fate only given the beasts forty-eight hours to claim their mates? What if Jaycee refused him? If his mate denied him anytime during the claiming, the bond wouldn't form. Wolf felt like he had the weight of the world on his shoulders at the moment, and time was not in his favor.

"I think it's a good idea to have Nikoli go with you," Nazaryth said. "Take Dog with you as well." The leader held up his hand when Wolf opened his mouth to protest. "With the hounds on the hunt for your mate, and the brimstone demons out there, you need backup. I will come along with you just in case the alpha is offended by us entering his territory."

He knew Nazaryth was thinking logically, even if Wolf wasn't, but he didn't like having an escort to go after his mate. He had tried half the night to reach his mate through their growing bond, but

Jaycee had never answered him. This not only frustrated Wolf, but it worried him as well.

The four used the exit in the living room and grabbed the Hummer. Wolf would have just flown, but it was early morning and too many humans were out.

The ride to Brac Village was agonizing and seemed to take forever. Wolf's need from the mating heat was becoming increasingly worse. His cock was so hard he was ready to whip it out in the truck and relieve the heavy burden, but he was pretty sure the other beasts would knock his ass out for jacking off in the car.

He honestly didn't care, but he would rather arrive conscious.

"How the hell did the little human make it all this way?" Dog asked from the passenger seat up front. "He must have been hauling ass."

Most times, Wolf appreciated Dog's bluntness, but not today. No, today the only thing Wolf would appreciate was feeling his mate in his arms. He had briefly held Jaycee in the hallway when Nikoli was too close, but that had been it. Wolf's arms hurt from the need to feel his mate fill them.

He blew out a breath and sat back, knowing it was going to be a long-ass ride.

* * * *

Jaycee opened his eyes to the blinding morning light streaming through a window. The window was pretty high up, but the sun had no problem shining past it and directly into Jaycee's eyes. Still, it looked like it might be early in the morning yet.

He groaned and covered his eyes, trying his best to block out the sun. Didn't this place believe in curtains? Even if the window was high up, it would help block out the damn sun. The sun wasn't going to budge, so Jaycee turned over, wanting more sleep. He was not expecting to see Wolf sitting on his ass, leaning back against the wall, with his arms resting on his bent knees. He looked as if he had lost his best friend as he sat there, staring at the floor.

Jaycee's heart ached to see the man look so lost. He hadn't meant to hurt Wolf, but Jaycee had been scared shitless from yesterday's events. Who wouldn't be? But he was also afraid because no man had ever flirted with Jaycee, or come on to him. Wolf was the first, and Jaycee was confused on how to handle Wolf's advances. He was confused about Wolf period.

"I come from a place called Zanthar. It isn't on any map, and can't be charted from any place on earth. It is a beautiful place to live, with sights so exotic, so glorious, that one's breath is taken away from just one glance. It needed to be guarded, to be protected from evil itself. And the gods decided that they would create such creatures to protect Zanthar. They created a race of beings to fight the hell hounds and any other vile creature that escaped hell. And so, I was created, not born."

Jaycee pushed up into a sitting position, brushing away his fallen hair from his face. Wolf's story intrigued him. Maybe if he knew the guy's story, he wouldn't be so afraid of him. He knew most fears came from the unknown, so Jaycee sat there and listened.

"I was exiled from that paradise."

"Why?" Jaycee asked before he could stop the words from leaving his lips.

Wolf's lip pulled back into a snarl, his head shaking back and forth slightly as he continued to stare at the floor. Jaycee wished the man would look at him. His heart began to ache for Wolf and what he lost, and he had never seen the place, but the hard lines on Wolf's face told Jaycee just what had been taken from the man.

"Because the new king feared the winged beasts." Wolf's hands fisted as anger marred his beautiful lips. "He was pure evil, Jaycee, and he knew we wouldn't stand idly by and watch him rule the kingdom that we cherished so much with an iron fist. He wanted us gone, the protectors of Zanthar, so he could rule any way he saw fit."

"He sounds like a real dickhead," Jaycee offered.

Wolf nodded. "He is."

"Is?"

"He still rules. Until he is replaced, we can never go home. We had no choice but to leave, so we came to the human realm, going into hiding, trying our best to stay off of his radar. He is the appointed king. He has been gifted with powers that make him superior to all others, even winged beasts."

"So how do those hounds and demons fit into all of this?" Jaycee was starting to see the hardship Wolf had endured. He wanted to go find that king and beat the snot out of him. No one should have to leave their home just because someone else wanted to be evil.

"The hounds were released by someone who envied us. Boromyr wanted eternal life. He wanted what he could never have, so he decided to sic the hounds on us." Wolf lifted his head, sorrow and pain in his pretty emerald-green eyes. "They can't be put back, Jaycee. If I could give you that one gift, I would. But once they are released, they can only be destroyed."

Jaycee slid from the bed and crawled over to Wolf, sitting in front of the man with his legs crossed. He wasn't sure why, but he felt an overwhelming need to be close to Wolf as he spilled his guts. "And the demons?"

"Every one hundred years, King Zephyr sends us a reminder that we are still banished and he still rules Zanthar. The brimstone demons are his reminder this time around."

"You have to admit, Wolf, that's a lot for a human like me to take in. It happened so fast, in such a short period of time that I freaked out. I'm used to working long hours and having car troubles, but your boss beats mine hands down in the asshole department."

An easy smile played at the corner of Wolf's mouth. "That he does."

Jaycee was growing to really like Wolf's smile. It softened the man's features and made him ten times more approachable. Jaycee scooted a little closer. He was amazed to see two dimples appear. He was right to think Wolf looked like a god. The man had an almost boyish charm about him as he sat there telling Jaycee all about his life.

"This is all just happening too fast, Wolf," Jaycee said as he laid his hand over one of Wolf's knees. "If I'm going to be living in your world, I need to know what I'm dealing with. Preferably before it shows up and tries to eat me."

Wolf turned his hand over, and Jaycee laid his hand in Wolf's. The winged vampire twined their fingers together and then gave them a little squeeze. "You really want to come back?"

Jaycee gave a slight shrug, staring at their entwined fingers. He admitted to himself that he liked holding Wolf's hand. It covered his and then some, but made him feel like everything was going to be all right. It was a strange feeling, but it started in his gut and began to spread throughout his body. Jaycee glanced up at Wolf to see the man smiling at him.

"If I went home, not only would the hounds be after me, but my life would be boring as hell after what I've witnessed." Jaycee pulled back slightly when Wolf closed his eyes, his face pinching as if he were fighting some inner turmoil. He wasn't sure if he should let the man's hand go. He decided to hold on. "Are you all right?"

Wolf breathed out a slow and steady breath, but Jaycee could see the sweat glistening on the man's golden skin. "I'll be fine," he said as he slowly opened his eyes. "Nothing to worry about."

Jaycee wasn't so sure, but he let it go. He wasn't one to pry. The man was probably just as tired as Jaycee was. He looked like he hadn't slept in days. "Truce?" he asked, unsure of where the word had come from.

"I want a truce with you, *zaterio*. I want so much with you. You have no idea of the bond that is forming between us, bringing us closer. Why do you fight it so much?" he asked.

Jaycee glanced down at his knees, wondering if he should tell Wolf. The beast hadn't done anything to Jaycee but show him kindness. The guy hadn't even come after him when Jaycee was hurling half the room at the man.

Maybe dating the guy wouldn't be so bad. "I've never had anyone interested in me before." Gods, he sounded like a loser. Wolf was probably wondering what was wrong with Jaycee that no one had been interested. "Not that there is anything wrong with me," he quickly defended as he blushed, glancing toward the hallway and wondering if he could outrun his embarrassment.

Wolf used their entwined hands to pull Jaycee closer until he was kneeling between Wolf's legs. "There is absolutely nothing wrong with you, *zaterio*."

Jaycee swallowed hard when Wolf cupped his face and pulled him forward. He was going to kiss Jaycee. It was in his eyes.

Jaycee's head snapped up when he heard loud arguing coming from the front of the center. He wasn't sure what in the hell was going on, but it sounded like a damn war was about to break out.

"Oh, hell," Wolf said as he pushed to his feet, pulling Jaycee along behind him.

* * * *

Wolf walked down the hallway pissed as hell. Not only had he just been robbed of his first kiss with his *zaterio*, but he could hear Nazaryth and Maverick arguing, their voices heated. He saw them standing in front of the resource center, looking murderously at each other. Wolf walked outside, Jaycee following.

"You promised not to tell him where Jaycee was!" Maverick shouted at Nazaryth, his canines extended. Wolf just hoped like hell they didn't go blow for blow. "You went against your word."

"Am I supposed to watch a man who has been under my command for two thousand years go mad because his mate is scared?

Would you do that to one of your pack members?" Nazaryth countered. "Wolf has not harmed his *zaterio*. Jaycee is just afraid of the world he has discovered around him. They'll work this out."

"How do you know this?" Maverick asked, his grey eyes so dark that they resembled chips of obsidian. Anger lines were formed all over the alpha's face, and his fists were balled so tight that his hands were turning white, with small lines of pink running through them. "He came to us for protection and you threw that back in our faces!"

"And if Jaycee tells him to go, we are here to make sure he leaves," Nazaryth said a little more calmly, his anger draining and exhaustion riding his face hard. Wolf knew that it was bad for the leaders to fight amongst themselves, and from the sigh Maverick released, the alpha must have come to the same conclusion.

"Wolf is feeling the mating heat very strongly right now. If he doesn't claim his *zaterio* within the allotted time, he will go mad, Maverick." Nazaryth's voice was almost pleading, which shocked the hell out of Wolf. He had never heard his commander beg anyone in two thousand years.

Nazaryth's mate didn't count.

The hand that Nazaryth pushed through his hair was agitated, ruffling his long black strands. "If he goes mad, then there is no coming back. A winged beast must be killed if he goes mad or there is no describing the havoc he will bring down upon us."

"Well, shit," Maverick cursed as he placed his hands on his hips, looking just as worried as Nazaryth.

"You could have filled me in on that small detail," Jaycee said as he yanked on Wolf's arm. "Is that why you're sweating?"

Wolf nodded, wincing when he got a good look at the fire burning in Jaycee's chocolate-brown eyes. "I didn't want to lay any more problems on your already-filled plate, *zaterio*. You have enough to take in as it is."

"Yeah, but none of it amounts to a hill of beans if you go nutty and have to be put down." Jaycee smacked Wolf in the arm. It didn't hurt, and Wolf didn't think it was meant to. But he got the message. "It's not okay to keep this stuff from me."

"*Zaterio*, I never meant—"

"I know what you meant!" Jaycee growled, doing a damn good impression of Wolf. "Now, you're going to go back into that room with me"—Jaycee pointed to the resource center—"and you are going to explain every last damn thing to me. Got it?"

Wolf's eyebrows shot up in surprise at the vehemence he could hear in Jaycee's voice. It coincided with the even further hardening of his already-hard cock. If Jaycee kept up this assertiveness, Wolf was likely to jump the man. He was hot as hell.

"Okay, *zaterio*, if that's what you wa—" Wolf froze, a thick chill entering his bones when a loud howl filled the air. He glanced over at Maverick. "Please tell me that's one of your wolves."

"Nope." Maverick was already pulling his cell phone out of his pocket as he shook his head. "My wolves know not to do that within the town limits unless it's an emergency."

"Dude, this might qualify." Wolf quickly turned to Jaycee and grabbed both of his hands. "*Zaterio*, I need you to go inside the center and stay inside. Avoid the windows, and whatever you hear, do not leave the building."

Jaycee frowned, his eyes level under drawn brows. "I'm not going to like this, am I?"

Oh hell, no, Jaycee wasn't going to like this one damn bit. "I think the hell dwellers have found us."

"Come with me," Jaycee said as he pulled on Wolf's hands, trying to draw him into the building. "We'll be safe inside, together."

"Jaycee, I can't." It killed Wolf inside to pull away from his mate, but he had no choice and he knew it. Wolf and the other winged beasts were the only thing standing between Jaycee and the hell hounds, and maybe the rest of Brac Village as well. "Please, *zaterio*, I need you to go inside where you'll be safe."

"What about you?"

"I have to stay here."

"Why?" Jaycee cried out.

"Fighting the hell dwellers is what I do, Jaycee. It's why I was created."

Wolf's heart was a heavy lump in his throat as he watched Jaycee and Taylor walk into the building, shutting the door behind them. He stared for a moment longer until Jaycee's shadow disappeared and then turned back to the others standing there.

Wolf wasn't sure which way the hell dwellers were coming from or even how many there were, but one was more than enough. One hell dweller could kill more innocent people than even Wolf cared to think about in a matter of minutes.

They were fast and they were vicious. And Wolf knew he had to stop them. His mate's life depended on it.

"How do you want to play this, Alpha? This is your town. You know it better than we do," Nazaryth asked as Dog and Wolf joined their commander.

"I've called my pack," Maverick said as he glanced around. "Backup is on the way."

"What about the humans?" Nazaryth asked. "It's still early in the morning, but people are going to start heading to work pretty soon. Any good ideas on how to keep them off the streets?"

"Zombie attack?" Dog asked.

Wolf snorted.

"No," Nazaryth said. "I've seen a zombie attack. They usually come in bigger groups than the hell dwellers. It's more like hordes."

Wolf's head snapped back in shock. "Really?"

"Hell, no!" Nazaryth rolled his eyes. "Zombies aren't real."

After the things Wolf had seen in his lifetime, he wouldn't place any bets on that. At this point, he wouldn't be surprised at anything he saw.

Except that.

"Oh shit, I think I'd rather face zombies," Wolf whispered to Dog as he watched three hell dwellers walk around the corner. That wouldn't have been so bad if they hadn't been flanking the two brimstone demons that attacked the castle earlier. All five of them looked pissed, too. At least he thought the demons looked pissed, but he wasn't really sure. Their faces already had a natural incline.

"Are those what I think they are?" Maverick asked in shock.

"Oh yeah," Nazaryth replied, "and we are so fucked!"

Dog chuckled evilly. "And they weren't even nice enough to bring lube, either."

Wolf extended his claws, ready for battle, sort of. Could someone actually ever really be ready for battle? He was scared to death. Scared that he wouldn't be able to defeat their enemies. Scared that he couldn't save his *zaterio*. Hell, he was just plain scared.

But he stood his ground. He had to. Not only was Jaycee's life was at stake, but Wolf didn't run from a goddamn thing—even if two of those things were ten feet fucking tall.

"Remember, Alpha," Nazaryth said as he took up his battle stance, "the only way to kill a hell dweller is to stab them in the mark behind their ear and then burn the bodies."

"And a demon?" Maverick asked.

"Let us handle them. You worry about your own ass."

As much as Wolf didn't want to change into his winged beast form out in public, he knew he wouldn't survive the demons' spit if he didn't fly.

"Watch their spit," Wolf warned the alpha.

"They spit?" Maverick asked as he snapped his head toward Wolf.

"Yeah, it's acid based. And watch their claws. They are deadly to any species."

"Fucking great," Maverick complained. "Remind me to thank the beasts properly after this is over…if we're still standing." He shifted into his timber wolf form right there on the street.

Wolf saw half a dozen trucks pull up, Maverick's pack climbing out. He sure as shit hoped it was Maverick's pack. Some men joined the fight, some blocked the street off. Wolf wasn't sure how effective that was going to be, but he prayed it worked.

"Hand him over," Morbius sneered at Wolf as he slowly sauntered toward him, his black hair flowing seamlessly behind him in the slight breeze. "I know you found your mate, beasty."

"Who sent you this time?" Nazaryth asked, pulling the long sword from the sheath running down his spine. "Boromyr is dead. Who is pulling your leash now, doggie?"

"No one is pulling my leash. King Zephyr decreed that all of the winged beasts' mates were to be killed when you pathetic excuses for men were exiled." Morbius tossed his head to the side as he laughed. "I guess you didn't know that, did you?"

Nope. Wolf hadn't a clue the king had done that. But fuck if any of them were getting their hands on his mate. Wolf would die to defend Jaycee—even if they were still on shaky ground.

"Surprise," Rythicam said with glee as he bounced excitedly beside Morbius. He was really tired of these two seasoned hell hounds. They were getting on Wolf's last nerve. "You know now."

"Just hand him over and we'll take the demons with us," Morbius added, casually waving a hand behind him. "I promise."

"Come get him," Wolf said as he unsheathed his sword as well. "Because you'll have to kill me first, prick."

Morbius grinned gleefully. "Done."

Wolf backed up, moving away from the center, drawing the hell hounds further down the street. He could see Nazaryth and Dog fighting the demons, the wolves trying to help but having to run every few seconds when the demons spit in their direction.

It was going to be a mass murder out here.

They were fighting things that could kill them without exerting themselves. As much as the timber wolves wanted to help, Wolf wasn't foolish enough to believe they could defeat two very large demons and three hounds with only three beasts and some wolves.

"Need help?"

Wolf wasn't sure who the newcomers were, but he was glad as fuck to see them.

"Don't let anyone scratch you, bite you, or spit at you," he warned before turning back to the hounds.

"Sounds like high school prom," the man said and then shifted into a...buffalo? Wolf shook his head, watching the others shift who had just joined them. He was shocked to see two cheetahs, a polar bear, two white Siberian tigers, a leopard, a rhino, and a coyote. What in the fuck was going on in this town? It was like a goddamn zoo.

"More to kill, goodie," Morbius said as he slapped his hands together and then rubbed them. "Let's do this, beasty."

The three hell hounds shifted into their Rottweiler forms, snapping and snarling as they tried their best to circle around Wolf and get closer to the resource center. The dogs were the biggest damn Rottweilers around, and weren't afraid to try and bite the shit out of someone with their larger-than-normal canines.

Wolf just prayed none of the timber wolves, or the zoo behind him, were bitten. He knew that everyone was a shifter, but that only meant that they had a fifty-fifty chance of surviving a bite, and zero if the demons did any damage.

Those odds weren't good enough for him.

Wolf flew up from the ground, ready to circle around the hounds when he felt like his entire lower half was on fire. He shouted, and glanced down at his leg to see his thigh muscle smoking. The pain was so excruciating that he nearly fell back down toward the ground.

"Wolf!" Nazaryth shouted, but Wolf waved him off. Even though he was sweating bullets and gritting his teeth from the demon's acid spit, he knew he had to stop the hounds from harming the shifters.

It wasn't easy though. His thigh felt like it was being branded by one hundred red-hot branding irons at the same time.

As he landed on his feet, the ground somehow came up quickly to greet him.

Chapter Six

"It's the nastiest shit I've ever seen," Dr. Nicholas Sheehan said as he closed the bedroom door quietly. "I think I tried everything in my arsenal to stop the demon spit from eating away his thigh muscle. After living among the paranormal for so long, I thought I had seen it all."

"And?" Nazaryth asked, feeling his patience wearing thin. He wanted to hear how Wolf was doing, not about the doctor's newest discovery.

Dr. Sheehan scratched at his jaw, looking totally baffled. This was not a good sign. Nazaryth had sent Dog back to the castle to grab the healing plants, and he knew Wolf wouldn't die from the venom in the spit, but it was some nasty-ass business. There was definitely going to be some scarring and possibly some muscle damage. The damage part was what worried him the most. Nazaryth had never seen one of his warriors take a hit like that before. None of them had ever gone down. If Wolf was permanently damaged, Nazaryth wasn't sure what he was going to do.

"And I've managed to stop the goop from eating any more of his skin. But there isn't anything I can do about the destroyed muscle without taking him to the hospital for surgery."

"You can't do that." Nazaryth sighed.

"No, I can't." Dr. Sheehan placed his hand on Nazaryth's arm, offering him a warm smile. "I'm sorry I couldn't do more."

Nazaryth could see the sincerity in the doctor's hazel eyes, but sincerity wasn't going to get Wolf up and walking again. He gave a nod to the doctor and then walked into the bedroom to see Wolf laid out on the bed with his upper thigh encased in gauze. Jaycee was sitting by the bed, his elbows resting on his thighs, his hands cupped together as if he were praying. The small human's eyes were glued to Wolf as he sat there silently.

Gods, how the roles were reversed now.

"When is he going to wake up?" Jaycee asked without looking away from Wolf.

Nazaryth wished he had an answer. He had never dealt with the venomous spit except dodging the vile goo. None of his warriors had ever been this badly damaged.

Until now.

"I'm not sure."

Jaycee dropped his hands, his head turning slowly as he glared hatefully toward Nazaryth. "I never asked to be in this world," he spat as he stood, his fists clenched at his sides. "But I'm here now. The only thing I had was Wolf, and now he may not recover?"

"You left him!" Nazaryth shouted before he could pull his anger under wraps. He couldn't believe Jaycee was basically accusing Nazaryth of getting Wolf hurt. He would do whatever he had to in order to ensure the safety of his beasts.

They had all been by his side in Zanthar and stuck together when exiled. There wasn't one damn thing Nazaryth wouldn't do for any of them, including taking Wolf's place right now. "Don't hold a mighty tongue with me, human. He was fighting to keep *you* safe."

Jaycee gasped and turned around, his shoulders slumping as he stared down at the bed. "I'm sorry."

Nazaryth wasn't sure if Jaycee was speaking to him or Wolf. He walked further into the room, standing on the opposite side of the bed as Wolf's mate. He ran a hand over his face, feeling sick to his stomach at the bandages covering the beast's upper leg. It wasn't supposed to be like this. King Zephyr wasn't supposed to win.

They were the good guys.

Good guys didn't lose.

"I didn't mean to yell at you," Jaycee said as he turned around, wiping at his eyes. "But Wolf is the first guy to ever take interest in me. And to be honest, it scared me, along with all the crazy monsters coming after me."

Shit. What was Nazaryth supposed to say to that?

"Knock, knock," Dog said as he walked into the bedroom, a small container with a lid in his hand. "I have what you wanted."

"Who are you?" Jaycee asked as he moved closer to Wolf, as if protecting the man. Nazaryth may have had hard feelings for the human when he left Wolf high and dry, but he could see that Jaycee was coming around. Wolf, along with the other beasts, deserved to find their *zaterios*, just like Nazaryth had. If Wolf's took a little longer acclimating to their world, Nazaryth wouldn't hold it against the human.

"I'm Dog," Dog said as he handed the paste over to Nazaryth. "And who are you?"

Jaycee stood a little straighter, jutting his chin out as he laid his hand on Wolf's, as if gaining some small measure of comfort by touching his mate. "I'm Jaycee, Wolf's Cheerio."

Nazaryth cocked his head at Jaycee as Dog began to laugh. "Cheerio, I like that."

"What do you have?" Jaycee asked as he nodded toward the container in Nazaryth's hand.

"It's a healing paste made of natural plants we grow," Nazaryth answered him. "And you are about to learn how to apply it."

"Me?" Jaycee asked, his voice wobbling as his brows shot straight up.

"Yes, you," Dog said this time. "If you are going to stick around and be Wolf's Cheerio"—Dog chuckled the word—"then you have to learn about winged beasts."

"Kind of like Wolf 101?"

"Something like that," Dog answered as Nazaryth handed Jaycee the bowl and showed the human how to spread the paste onto Wolf's leg. Nazaryth gagged and his stomach lurched when he removed the bandage. The wound had already been cleaned by the doctor, but it was still a very nasty mess. The skin looked as though it had been put through a meat grinder, and there were black spots that looked as if they had been burnt to a crisp. He wasn't sure if Wolf would even have full use of his leg after this.

Nazaryth was extremely impressed when Jaycee didn't even wince, but listened to everything Nazaryth told him, nodded, and then grabbed the paste and applied it until the container was empty.

"Now what?" Jaycee asked as he set the container down. He glanced up at Nazaryth, waiting.

"Rebandage his leg, Jaycee." Nazaryth grinned as he handed the human the fresh bandages. "Be careful not to—" Nazaryth winced when Jaycee bumped Wolf's leg and Wolf's eyes flew open.

"Fuck!" Wolf screamed as he grabbed his leg and then yelled again.

"Let go of your leg!" Jaycee shouted as he struggled to get Wolf's fingers from being curled around the paste.

"Wolf!" Nazaryth snapped the one word loudly and the beast immediately let go. He was the winged beasts' commander. The very first beast created. All other beasts listened to his commands. They were built that way. He normally didn't use the commanding tone to get what he wanted, but Wolf had been trying to claw the skin from his leg.

"Lay back while I bandage you!" Jaycee said in a no-nonsense tone as he knocked Wolf's hand away. Dog snickered as Nazaryth curled his lips in, hiding his smile.

"Just don't smack my leg again," Wolf gritted out.

"Sorry, that was an accident. I'm new at this, okay?" Jaycee's voice had turned soothing as he rubbed his hand over Wolf's arm. "Lay back so I can get this done."

Wolf's eyes shot over to Nazaryth, his expression pleading. Nazaryth held his hands up and shook his head as he backed away. Wolf glowered at him.

"Suck it up," Dog teased.

"Suck this up." Wolf flipped Dog off.

"Behave," Jaycee scolded Wolf as he began to bandage Wolf's injury.

Nazaryth shook his head, amazed at Jaycee and how he had set aside his fears and handled his business. He had nothing but respect for the human now.

"Come on," Nazaryth said to Dog. "We have a village to put back together."

"And some bodies to burn," Dog reminded him a little too gleefully.

* * * *

Jaycee was a nervous wreck. Not only was he terrified he would bump Wolf's injury again, but something had snapped inside of him when he was told Wolf was badly injured. Jaycee had thought his heart would stop beating.

He couldn't understand the attraction he had to the man. It was crazy. It was confusing. And Jaycee knew he was an idiot for sticking around all of this madness. But he couldn't deny that the longer he stuck around Wolf, the stronger the attraction he felt.

His head was still reeling from finding out that Wolf would go mad if he didn't fuck Jaycee. That wasn't something Jaycee ran into every day. He didn't want Wolf to go mad and have to be killed, but damn. Why him? Jaycee just couldn't understand how he was picked for Wolf out of the billions of people who inhabited the earth.

He knew Wolf said they were mates, but Jaycee still had a hard time believing any of this existed.

"Stop shaking," Wolf said as he placed his hand on Jaycee's. He hadn't even been aware that his hands were trembling.

"I'm just afraid of hurting you again," Jaycee admitted as he blew out a steady breath and began to bandage Wolf's leg once more.

"The only way you can hurt me is by leaving again."

Ouch. Talk about straight to the point. Jaycee hadn't a clue what to say. He had felt justified in leaving, but when Wolf reminded him of the fact that he had left, it hurt like hell.

"Come here." Wolf held his hand out, and Jaycee took it. "Sit down."

Jaycee carefully took a seat, making sure he didn't accidently bump Wolf's leg again.

"I didn't say that to hurt you. I just wanted you to know what could cripple me, *zaterio*. I never want to hurt you, ever." Wolf reached up and pushed Jaycee's hair aside, rubbing his thumb over Jaycee's cheek. "You were created just for me. Did you know that?"

"No," Jaycee whispered as he stared into Wolf's sparkling green gems. "How do you know that?"

"Because, the gods told me."

Jaycee wasn't too sure about *the gods* telling Wolf anything, but he had witnessed some very strange things in the past two days. He wouldn't doubt that what Wolf was telling him was the truth. Now that Jaycee wasn't freaking out and was thinking things through, he realized that—just as long as no one was trying to attack him—he liked being with Wolf. The man was easygoing, caring, and nice to look at. Wolf was someone Jaycee would like to get to know better. He wasn't like anyone Jaycee had ever met before, personality wise, not the whole otherworldly thing.

Wolf grinned up at Jaycee with a heart-stopping smile. "I told you, I was created, not born as you were."

"And they told you that I was created for you? I wasn't even born two thousand years ago," he pointed out.

Wolf chuckled. "No, you weren't. The gods told the winged beasts that we would know when we found our mates, that we would feel it in the very depths of our bones. You will be granted only one mate, and he will be referred to as the chosen one," Wolf said as if reciting something he had heard, running his fingers over Jaycee's cheeks the entire time. "And you, my Cheerio, are my chosen one."

Jaycee was panting heavily as Wolf pulled him forward, brushing his lips across Jaycee's. It was soft, tentative, as if Wolf was waiting for Jaycee to give the go-ahead. His mind was telling him that he needed to pull back, that this was insane, but Jaycee wasn't sure if he could pull back. As much as he wanted things to slow down, another part of him, the lower half of course, was screaming for him to move full steam ahead. Jaycee wasn't sure which to listen to, so he ignored them both and sealed his lips over Wolf's.

Wolf didn't pull him down or become dominating as Jaycee would have thought. The kiss remained simmering, with just an edge of desire. Jaycee scooted a little closer, and wound his fingers into Wolf's hair. It felt as soft as it looked. He found his fingers had a mind of their own as they rubbed through the silky strands as Jaycee licked Wolf's bottom lip.

"I am wounded, yet I cannot stop thinking of taking you."

Jaycee heard Wolf's voice in his head, but didn't let it freak him out this time. He was kind of growing used to it. And in a small way, it was becoming comforting. But the thought of letting Wolf have him was a bit intimidating. The man wasn't small in any form.

"Slow down." Jaycee pushed the thought into Wolf's head. *"Please,"* he added.

Wolf grinned into Jaycee's mouth as he nipped his bottom lip. "I know you need time, *zaterio*. I would give you all the time in the world—"

"But you're on a deadline."

Wolf nodded.

Jaycee pulled back enough to look into Wolf's pretty green eyes. He could see small flecks of black that he had never noticed before. The coloring was amazing. "How long until you lose your mind?"

"Twenty-four hours."

Jaycee closed his eyes and sighed. "That's not enough time, Wolf."

"I know."

Chewing his bottom lip, Jaycee glanced up at the man. "I tell you what. Can you handle twelve more hours?"

Wolf shrugged, brushing back Jaycee's hair from his eyes. The man seemed to love touching Jaycee's hair. "I'm not sure. I've never gone through the mating heat before. But it will only get worse the longer you are left unclaimed."

Geez. It had a name? Why did it have to be called *mating heat*? It sounded like something a cat went through. "Okay, maybe twelve hours might not cut it, but I don't want to say yes and then end up with an asshole."

Wolf laughed as he cupped Jaycee's face. "I have shown you my true self, *zaterio*. But if you want to see my beast, I can show it to you."

"The funky green thing you changed into when you left the living room to go fight the demons?" Yeah, Jaycee remembered Wolf's beast. It had freaked him out at the time, so he pretended he hadn't really seen it. If he was going to stick around and be Wolf's mate, then Jaycee needed to start accepting things around him, even The Incredible Hulk. His feelings were growing stronger toward a man he had just met yesterday, and Jaycee couldn't understand that, but there was no denying that he had felt a great loss when he had left Wolf.

"That would be my beast, yes. Our coloring all depends on our age and our rank. Nazaryth's beast is red because he is our commander. My green coloring indicates that I was one of the *zenyons* of our group of twelve."

"What is that?"

"In translation, it means that I was responsible for guarding the king as he slept. Trap and Tyson also had that honor as well. It was the highest honor a king could bestow on a winged beast. They put their lives in our hands as they closed their eyes and rested. But that was before Zephyr took over. He banished anyone from his bedchamber. He didn't trust us."

"I can see why," Jaycee commented. "But if you guys were created, wouldn't you be the same age?"

"No, it takes one hundred years to create a winged beast. The process is long and involves a great deal. Not all have survived their creation. I was created four hundred years after Nazaryth."

Jaycee felt as though Wolf was telling him some sort of fairy tale. It didn't seem possible that all of this was real. But it had to be because Wolf was lying right here on the bed. "I'm scared as hell, Wolf. From what I gather, once you claim me, that's it. There is no going back." And Jaycee wasn't sure what he would do if Wolf turned out to be an asshole. The winged vampire had found him at the center. Was there nowhere he could run if he wanted to escape the man?

"If you refuse me anytime during the claiming, the bond will not form. You are my only chance at happiness, Jaycee. I would never risk harming you. I would be the greatest fool alive to do such a thing."

Pretty words, but did the man mean them? "If you turn out to be an ass, what can I do about it?"

"Tell Nazaryth," Wolf said with dark heat in his voice. The man's face was fierce as he stared at Jaycee. "Nazaryth would torture me for a millennium if I hurt you in *any* way. He, along with all winged beasts, knows how precious a *zaterio* is. They are to be treasured, not abused. You will understand once we are mated that it is you who has the power in this relationship. You are the sole person who holds my heart, *zaterio*."

Gods, Jaycee wanted to say yes. He honestly did, but he was so damn scared to put his trust in another's hands. He would live in this world, be a part of it. He would deal with hell hounds and anything else that came his way. Could he do that? Could he endure whatever came after him just to be with Wolf?

"Do you refuse me, Jaycee?"

"I don't want to."

"Then come to me, mate," Wolf said as he lay there. Jaycee was waiting for Wolf to pull him closer, but Wolf didn't move. Maybe the man was afraid Jaycee would resist. He did say that if Jaycee refused him anytime during the claiming, it wouldn't work.

Jaycee placed his hand on Wolf's broad chest, wondering what he should do. "How does this work?"

"I will claim you with the core of my being," Wolf said as he turned onto his side, pulling Jaycee down next to him. "I am injured, so I will not be as graceful for you."

Jaycee really didn't care about Wolf being graceful. "The only thing I care about is you taking your time with me." He couldn't believe he had said that out loud.

* * * *

"I plan on taking my time, *zaterio*. I plan on exploring every inch of your sexy body," he murmured as he ran his hand down Jaycee's side until he felt the hem of his mate's shirt. He slid his fingers under the material and shuddered at the feel of his mate's silky, soft skin under his fingers.

Wolf leaned in closer, inhaling his mate's scent. His beast shifted around inside of Wolf, a growl rumbling in a place that was deep inside Wolf, telling him that the claiming had begun. "It has begun, *zaterio*. If you refuse me now, we will not be bound together."

Jaycee's eyes lifted until they met Wolf's, his small pink tongue flickering out and wetting his lips. "I don't want to refuse you, Wolf."

Wolf could see the sincerity in the depths of Jaycee's dark-brown eyes, eyes that had begun to darken with desire. He prayed Jaycee spoke the truth. The man had been running from him since he had opened his eyes yesterday. Wolf was afraid, but it was too late. The claiming was unfolding right there between them. His cock was full and pulsing in his jeans, begging to be released.

"I may need help undressing." One leg of his jeans had been cut off to care for his wound, but the doctor had left his pants on.

Jaycee's eyes widened, and then he glanced down at Wolf's pants, a blush stealing across his cheeks as he nodded his head, a wisp of hair falling across his mate's face. Wolf reached up and tucked it behind Jaycee's ear. He loved how his mate's hair felt. He could play with it for hours.

Jaycee placed his hand on Wolf's chest, guiding him to his back. Wolf's wings spanned out, fluttering wildly in anticipation of claiming the human. Jaycee crawled between Wolf's legs and unsnapped his pants. Wolf could see his mate's fingers shaking slightly.

He didn't say a word. He allowed Jaycee to take as much time as he needed. His *zaterio* had asked Wolf to go slow, and he would. He would give his mate anything he wanted and more. He was Wolf's happiness, and Wolf wasn't going to screw this up.

"You have to lift your hips," Jaycee said. "But do it carefully."

Wolf held back the hiss as Jaycee pulled the rough denim over his wound. He didn't want Jaycee to call a stop to this because he was worried about Wolf's leg. Even with good intentions, Wolf feared that by stopping, the bond would be lost to them forever.

Jaycee tossed Wolf's jeans aside and then helped him pull his shirt over his head. Wolf lay there naked, his cock ramrod straight and pulsing against his stomach. Jaycee just knelt there for a moment, staring at it with liquid heat blazing in his eyes.

"As much as I love you staring at my body, I'd like to see yours," Wolf said and then reached for Jaycee's shirt. Jaycee lifted his arms and his shirt was tossed aside. Wolf ran his hand over Jaycee's sinewy stomach, feeling the hard, flat planes under his fingers. He reached up and brushed his thumbs over his mate's nipples, smiling lightly when Jaycee shivered and his nipples turned into two hard pebbles.

Jaycee leaned away from Wolf's touch. He frowned until he saw his mate shucking his pants. A blaze of lust flared inside of Wolf when Jaycee's cock sprang free, the head already an angry red. His mate's body was slim, pale, and so gorgeous that Wolf almost whimpered to be inside of his mate.

Jaycee released his jeans over the side of the bed and then stared down at Wolf from the fall of his bangs. The prolonged anticipation was almost unbearable. Wolf reached a hand behind Jaycee's head and fisted his mate's hair, bringing him down as Wolf claimed Jaycee's lips. Wolf's calm was shattered with the hunger building up inside of him. His wings fanned and his cock became impossibly harder.

The touch of Jaycee's lips against his was a heady sensation that Wolf was now addicted to. He wasn't used to feeling a goatee scraping against his skin, but he knew he could kiss Jaycee for hours on end and never tire of the man's sweet taste. The rough rasp of Jaycee's goatee only added pleasure to the already-explosive kiss. Wolf grabbed the length between his fingers and gave a light tug. Jaycee moaned and parted his lips, and pleasure radiated outward as Wolf's tongue swept into the moist, cavernous mouth of his *zaterio*.

Jaycee's hands skimmed over Wolf's chest until his fingers began to play with Wolf's nipples. He groaned at the sensation. Wolf's legs parted, and he pulled his mate between them, their cocks brushing against one another, making Wolf's thoughts spin out of control. Feeling their skin touch unhindered was more exquisite than Wolf even dreamed it would be.

His mate broke the kiss and scooted down Wolf's chest, taking one lone nipple into his mouth. Wolf hissed, running his fingers through Jaycee's dark hair, gently scraping his nails over his mate's scalp.

Jaycee closed his lips over the peak and then gently bit Wolf's flesh, rolling the nub around with his teeth. A growl ripped from Wolf's throat. The caress of his lips on Wolf's body sent Wolf up into flames.

"*Zaterio*, you torture my body so sweetly."

Jaycee gazed up at Wolf, his swollen lips parting in a smile. Wolf growled at the erotic portrait his mate painted and grabbed the man, pulling him up until Jaycee was straddling his hips. Jaycee's cock jutted out and Wolf wrapped his fingers around the heated flesh. His mate moaned as his head rocked back on his shoulder as Wolf began to slowly stroke his mate.

"You are mine for all eternity, Jaycee. I will never let you go. You are my *zaterio*, my chosen one." Wolf reached behind his mate with his free hand and circled his mate's tight ring of muscles, dipping the tip of his finger inside and then pulling free. He reached over to the nightstand and prayed there was some lube inside the drawer. He wasn't in his bedroom after all.

He snagged the bottle and released Jaycee's cock, spreading the clear gel onto both hands and then dropping the bottle. He used one lubed hand to stroke his mate's straining erection while the other made its way back to Jaycee's ass.

"Lean forward."

Jaycee pressed his hands into Wolf's chest, his breath coming out quicker as he stared down at Wolf with so much trust and desire that Wolf felt his heart seize in his chest from the emotions tightening his chest.

Sliding one finger into Jaycee's ass, Wolf gripped his mate's cock harder, their eyes never straying from each other.

"That feels so damn good, Wolf," Jaycee moaned. "Add another finger."

Wolf obliged his mate, slipping a second one in next to the first. He hated that he was wounded. Wolf wanted to show Jaycee his stamina, his prowess as he mated the man. But he knew that he had limited mobility at the moment.

Jaycee leaned forward and nipped Wolf's chin, his tongue skimming across Wolf's jaw. Wolf's chest began to rise and fall more quickly now, the head of his cock brushing Jaycee's ass and throbbing with need.

His *zaterio* brushed a featherlight kiss across Wolf's lips, grinning. "I thought your lips would be hard, but they're soft and warm."

"Why?" Wolf asked, "Because I am a warrior?"

Jaycee nodded.

"There are many places on my body that are hard, *zaterio*." Wolf hitched his hips, his cock stabbing into Jaycee's ass cheek. "But my lips are not one of them."

Wolf speared a third finger into Jaycee's ass and moaned at how silky his mate's channel was. It sucked his fingers in greedily as Wolf stretched his fingers apart, twisting his wrist and looking for Jaycee's hot spot.

"Wolf!"

Wolf had found it, and stroked his fingers over the walnut-sized gland over and over again until his mate's arms began to shake.

"When I am healed, I will show you many more ways your body can sing with pleasure from my touch."

"O–Okay," Jaycee said as he swallowed hard.

Wolf pulled his hand free, grabbed Jaycee's hips, and rolled so quickly that he bit his bottom lip to keep the howl of pain trapped behind them. He pushed the pain aside, shoved it deep down inside of him, and locked it away as best he could so he could claim his mate properly.

"Wolf—"

"My *zaterio*," Wolf growled and then lined his cock up to Jaycee's well-lubed hole. "My mate." He thrust forward, Jaycee crying out as Wolf's wings spanned out to their five-foot length. They began fluttering and fanning, the mating dust falling on them like fresh, new snow. It was light, as light as fine dust, but it was a part of the ritual that would bind them for all eternity.

"You have wings!" Jaycee shouted as his fingers dug into Wolf's chest, the nails breaking skin and drawing blood. Wolf growled, pressing his chest harder against his mate's fingers. He welcomed the pain. It was barbaric and savage and only heightened the sensations of claiming his mate.

"You did call me a winged vampire, *zaterio*," Wolf teased.

"But I didn't think—oh hell," Jaycee's head rolled back and forth against the pillow as he pulled his legs further back into his chest. "You feel so damn good inside of me."

Wolf applied the weight of his body into his good leg, stretching out the wounded one and keeping as much pressure off of it as possible. He thrust his cock deeply into Jaycee's ass, feeling it swell even further as his mate's cock bounced freely between them. His mouth watered to taste his mate, but Wolf was too lost in the feeling of being inside the human to pull free.

"My *zaterio*," Wolf growled and then sank his fangs into Jaycee's neck. The sweet taste of his mate's blood splashed over his tongue as Wolf drank from his mate, feeding the vampire in him and sating one of his needs.

As Wolf drank he saw his creation, along with Jaycee's birth. Their two lives raced alongside each other at the speed of light as they played out until they crashed and intertwined, forever binding them together.

Jaycee cried out, his cock exploding between them, wetting both of their bodies with his seed. "How can I see your creation?" he asked in shock. "How can I feel you in my mind, my soul, my damn heart, Wolf?"

Wolf pulled his fangs free, licking the wound closed. "Because you are mine!" he roared, and then he fell backward over the edge of the abyss, tumbling down as his body convulsed with his release. He shuddered and jerked, and then pulled free of Jaycee's body, rolling, taking his mate with him as he landed on his back, wrapping his mate in his wings.

"This is impossible," Jaycee whispered. "You have wings, and I saw your life play out in my mind."

"That was the binding, *zaterio*. It showed us our lives before we were joined, how lonely we were, until I claimed you, and then it joined the very fibers of our beings together. Never again will be we be two entities, but one."

Jaycee curled into Wolf's side, sighing contently. "I like that, Wolf," he said softly. "I like belonging to you."

As much of a fight as Jaycee had put up about belonging to Wolf, those whispered words meant more to him than Jaycee would ever truly know.

Chapter Seven

Wolf hissed as he woke, feeling the pain throbbing in his leg. Never again in his eternal life did he want to feel pain like this again. It was like a toothache and being hit by a bus all rolled into one.

He stilled when he felt a warm heat against his side. He glanced down to see his mate curled into his side, fast asleep. Wolf smiled as he brushed Jaycee's long black hair from his face and remembered last night. It had been one of the best nights he had ever had. The claiming had been even more amazing than what Nazaryth had described to them. His commander hadn't told Wolf that he would feel a connection so deep that he could feel it in his very bones.

Careful not to jostle his leg too much, Wolf turned onto his side, staring down at the stunning man. Truth be told, the man was the star of every fantasy Wolf had ever had. He just hadn't known it was Jaycee starring in them until he had set eyes on his mate. And last night had been every damn fantasy come true.

He nuzzled his mate, inhaling his scent, and then licked his tongue over the twin pinpricks that were already healed. *What a pity.* Wolf would have loved to see Jaycee walk around with his mark.

"No licking the Cheerio first thing in the morning," Jaycee grumbled as he turned over, pressing his very tempting and tight little ass into Wolf's groin. If Jaycee didn't like morning sex, then he should keep his nice round tush away from Wolf's growing erection. It was like waving a red flag in front of a bull. Wolf would take the challenge happily.

"Don't even think about it," Jaycee warned as he burrowed deeper into Wolf's side. "My ass is still sore as hell."

Wolf grinned as he pulled his hips away from the temptation and kissed the side of Jaycee's ear. "Morning, mate."

"Five more minutes, Ma," Jaycee groaned. "I'm not a morning person, yet you keep insisting on waking me up at the crack of dawn. What's a guy gotta do around here to sleep in?"

Wolf had many ideas, but he knew Jaycee didn't want to hear them. They ranged from a quick blow job to his *zaterio* performing acrobatics as Wolf fucked him back into sleep.

"We need to get up, Jaycee. We have a very long drive ahead of us," he reminded his mate, waiting for Jaycee to turn over so he could look into the man's pretty brown eyes once more. Wolf could get used to waking up like this. It was like having a piece of heaven handed to him first thing in the morning.

Jaycee groaned, and then rolled to his stomach, his naked ass in plain sight for Wolf to salivate over. "Can I go back to sleep on the way home?"

Wolf nodded as he carefully slid from the bed, hissing when he put pressure on his injured leg. He wasn't used to dealing with this much pain. It was irritating as hell. "Since I can't drive, Dog will be taking us back. You can sleep in the back of the Hummer."

"What about Rico's car?" Jaycee asked as he pulled the sheet around him, covering his naked form. If Jaycee was shy about being seen naked, the man was going to have a rude awakening. Wolf planned on seeing that beautiful body every chance he could get.

"Nazaryth will drive it back."

Jaycee wrapped the sheet around him as he slid from the bed, heading toward the bathroom. Wolf grinned as he reached out and grabbed the sheet, snatching it out of Jaycee's grasp. "Nice."

His *zaterio* blushed seven shades of red as he hurried to the bathroom. Wolf thought it was endearing as hell. He had to use the sheet to wrap around his waist when someone knocked on the door. Limping, Wolf crossed the room to answer it. It was the shifter doctor.

"Good morning," Dr. Sheehan said as he stood on the other side of the door. "I came to check your leg before you headed out."

Wolf walked slowly, and painfully, to the bed and sat down, pulling the sheet aside. His leg was killing him.

"I'll need you to lie down so I can remove the bandages and see what we're dealing with."

Wolf scooted onto the bed. From the pain radiating in his leg, it was any wonder he had claimed Jaycee last night. His thigh was throbbing so bad that Wolf would rather take on one hundred hell hounds than endure this shit another minute.

When the bathroom door opened, Wolf sat up. "Stay inside, *zaterio*. The doctor is here."

Dr. Sheehan chuckled as he unwrapped Wolf's leg. "I've seen naked men before, Wolf. Your mate can dress. I pinky promise not to turn around."

Wolf glanced at Jaycee's clothes on the floor. "Can you place his clothes by the bathroom door?" That was more acceptable to Wolf than his mate dressing in the room with another man present. That thought alone made Wolf see red.

"Sure," the doctor said as he grabbed Jaycee's clothes and deposited them by the door. "Your clothes are on the floor right outside the door."

Wolf smiled when Jaycee's arm appeared and the clothes were snatched up, the door slamming quickly closed.

"Shy?" Dr. Sheehan asked as he finished removing the bandage. Wolf ignored the question. He wasn't going to discuss his mate's shyness with anyone. He glanced down at his leg when it was bared, and he grimaced. Damn, it looked a fucking mess. The skin on his outer thigh, right below his hip, looked like it was melted. He couldn't shift and heal like a shifter, so Wolf knew he was going to have a nasty scar once the wound did heal.

"I don't see any pus or draining. I think you're safe from infection, but I'd like to give you some antibiotics just to be on the safe side."

He gritted his teeth from the raw pain that shot through his entire body as he watched Dr. Sheehan clean the wound. Fuck, it hurt! "Antibiotics won't work with me," he said between clenched teeth.

"Normally, I would agree," Dr. Sheehan said as he used a strangely shaped sponge to clean away the dead skin and then irrigated the wound. Wolf wanted to howl it hurt so damn bad. "But Dr. Carmichael has come up with something that has worked on some paranormal creatures with success. I want you to try it."

Wolf was willing to try anything if the man would stop touching his damn leg. Jaycee came out of the bathroom with his jeans and shirt on, crossed the room, and climbed onto the bed, opposite the doctor. "How is he?"

"He'll live, but he'll be scarred. I'm going to give you some supplies to take home with you, Jaycee. I want you to keep an eye on his wound. If it gets any worse, I want you to call Dr. Samuel at Pride Pack Valley General. He'll know what to do."

Jaycee nodded as he grabbed Wolf's hand, holding it in his lap as he watched the doctor finish torturing Wolf and then rebandage his leg.

"I'll give you a sheet with instructions on them that will tell you how to clean his wound and what to look for as far as infection goes."

Jaycee nodded quickly as the doctor spoke, his eyes trained on what Dr. Sheehan was doing to Wolf's leg. Wolf felt tenderness wrap around his heart that Jaycee would even consider tending to his wound. His *zaterio* looked nervous as hell, but paid attention to what the doctor was saying.

"Can you give me your phone number in case I have any questions?" Jaycee asked.

"Sure." Dr. Sheehan reached into his back pocket, extracted his wallet, and handed Jaycee a business card. "My cell number is at the bottom."

"Is he okay to travel?" Jaycee asked as he tucked the card into his back pocket.

"Yes, but I wouldn't allow him to do anything strenuous until his leg has healed."

Jaycee blushed and Wolf chuckled.

"Anything else strenuous," the doctor said as he winked at Jaycee. "No more hanky-panky until his leg is better. Once he gets home, make sure he gets plenty of rest." The doctor turned toward Wolf. "Once you are up to it, you can start some physical therapy if needed. I've already called Dr. Samuel and given him a heads-up, so he'll be looking for your call."

Wolf didn't want to see any more doctors. He was fine. A few days of rest and he would be as good as new. Demon spit was not going to keep him down.

"He'll get his rest," Jaycee assured the doctor.

Wolf could imagine all sorts of ways Jaycee could keep him company in bed, although he was sure they went against the doc's orders.

"Do that. I'll have some supplies ready for you by the time you guys leave."

Wolf and Jaycee thanked the doctor as he left.

"How are you going to keep me in bed?" Wolf asked as he wiggled his brows and reached for his mate. He gaped at Jaycee when the man batted his hand away.

"You heard the doctor. No fooling around until your leg is healed. The mating heat is gone, so I think you'll be just fine."

"Seriously?" Wolf asked. "You're going to deny me because the doctor said so?"

Jaycee chuckled. "Stop whining. You'll be all right. I don't think a week without sex will kill you."

"A week!" Gods, he was newly mated. There was no way he was waiting an entire week to have Jaycee back under him. He was hard-pressed not to have the man now. Wolf dropped his head onto the pillow, groaning as he stared up at the ceiling.

"I'll go make sure everything is ready while you rest," Jaycee said as he pushed from the bed. "Don't get up."

"Wouldn't dream of it," Wolf grumbled.

Jaycee grinned as he walked around the bed. "Stop pouting. This is for your own good, Wolf."

"Then give me a kiss."

Jaycee shook his head. "I know where a kiss will lead."

"Fine," he said as he waved toward the door. "Go see Dog and ask him when I'm getting the hell out of here." He was being a big baby, and he knew it. But the thought of Jaycee turning him down soured his mood.

"I'll be back." Jaycee left the room.

"I'm going to get some ass," he promised himself out loud as he turned over, wincing from the pain. "Just as soon as my leg heals."

* * * *

Jaycee stood outside the bedroom door and wondered where he could find Dog. This place was huge. He had glanced around the home yesterday when he was brought here, but he had been so worried about Wolf that he hadn't paid that much attention.

"Do you need help?" a slim man asked as he walked toward Jaycee. "You look a little lost."

"I'm looking for Dog."

The guy scratched his chin. "Is he one of the winged beasts I keep hearing about?"

Jaycee nodded.

"Then we should probably go ask Maverick. He knows everything that goes on around here."

Jaycee shrugged and followed the man down a grand staircase. The place was decked out. He wasn't sure whose home was nicer, this one or Wolf's. They were both very posh. He noticed the man kept looking over his shoulder at Jaycee. "Is there something wrong?"

"No, nothing at all. I've just never seen a winged beast before," the man said quickly. "By the way, I'm Murphy."

"Jaycee."

"Can you show me what a winged beast looks like?" Murphy asked. "Just as long as he isn't armed, that is."

Jaycee cocked his head. What the hell did that mean?

"Never mind. I can't take the time right now anyway. I have a soap to watch. If you follow this hallway, you'll find Maverick's office on your right."

"Thanks," Jaycee said, glancing at the strange man once more before heading down the hallway. And he thought his roommates were loony? Jaycee was relieved when he spotted Dog and Nazaryth standing in the hallway with Maverick. He hadn't been looking forward to searching the place.

"How is Wolf?" Nazaryth asked.

"Better, but his leg is going to need time to heal." Jaycee slowly approached the men. They were pretty damn big, especially the one that looked like a biker man. He usually wasn't intimidated, but knowing these men weren't human didn't help his nerves.

"Did the doctor clear him to travel?" Dog asked.

"He's cleared, but was told not to do anything strenuous."

Dog chuckled, as if he already knew the inside joke. Jaycee was embarrassed as hell that any of them knew what he and Wolf had done. Not that he would deny Wolf, but he didn't want to sit down and have tea and talk about it either.

"It'll be a smooth ride," Dog promised. "Nazaryth and I will get Wolf down here. You can wait in the foyer."

Jaycee nodded and then turned toward Maverick. "Thank you for helping...with all of it."

"You are welcome, Jaycee." Maverick watched Jaycee with those eerie grey eyes until Dog and Nazaryth were gone, and then he leaned against the wall, crossing his arms over his large chest. "Are you going to run again?"

"I hadn't planned on it, but if you're asking if I will bring more trouble to your town, the answer is no."

"I can handle my town, as you saw. What I want you to know is that finding a mate for any species is very rare. I would think long and hard the next time you panic and run." Maverick pushed from the wall and walked into the room behind him, leaving Jaycee to stand in the hallway by himself.

He wasn't going to feel guilty for running. But he did hate the fact that trouble had followed him. The people in this town had been nice enough to extend their hands, and Jaycee had brought the hounds and demons to their doorstep.

He was ready to get out of here.

"I can walk!"

Jaycee hurried down the hall when he heard Wolf shouting. He had never heard the man yell like that before. He wasn't sure who his mate was yelling at, but Jaycee knew he needed to see what was going on.

"Fine, idiot." Dog snapped a reply at Wolf and then moved away. Jaycee yelped when Wolf began to fall forward, but Dog caught him in time before his face smacked against the floor. "Have I made my point?"

"Fuck you," Wolf growled as Dog chuckled. Nazaryth grabbed Wolf's other side, his expression grim as they began to carefully walk Wolf toward the door. Jaycee ran for the door, opening it so they could walk Wolf through unhindered.

"Can you open the door to the Hummer?" Nazaryth asked.

"Sure." Jaycee stepped outside and looked around, making sure there were no creatures with the word *hell* attached to their name before darting across the lawn and opening the back door to the truck.

"Don't touch my ass," Wolf barked at Dog.

"I didn't!"

"I know you too well," Wolf replied.

"You better be lucky I didn't kick your ass into the truck," Dog mumbled as he stepped back and slammed the door. "If he doesn't stop bitching like an old woman, I'm going to knock him unconscious. Hell if I'm listening to that shit all the way home."

Jaycee ran back to the house and grabbed the bag Dr. Sheehan had left by the front door for Wolf. He prayed as he ran back to the truck that Wolf didn't piss Dog off. The man was their ride home, after all.

"Take me to town so I can drive the other vehicle home," Nazaryth said as Jaycee climbed into the back of the truck.

"Will do, boss," Dog replied as he started the truck and pulled from the gravel drive. Jaycee was glad to get out of there. He wasn't sure about the castle they were headed to, but since he was mated to Wolf now, he was going to have to get used to it.

"Thank you for helping," Jaycee said from the backseat.

Nazaryth nodded.

Jaycee sat back, blowing out a long breath. He knew the winged guys were mad at him for leaving. All sorts of crap had happened from that one decision. He regretted what happened, but damn it, he was scared. What part of that didn't they understand?

"I can feel your anger, zaterio. *What's wrong?"* Wolf pulled Jaycee closer, tucking him into the side of his body.

"Everyone is mad at me."

"Are you mad at my mate?" Wolf asked the men up front.

Jaycee gaped at Wolf and then smacked him in the chest. "You weren't supposed to ask them!"

"Then how will you know?"

"No one is mad at you, Jaycee," Dog replied. "We were worried, but not mad."

"It is a lot for a human to take in," Nazaryth added. "At least my mate already knew about the paranormal world even if he didn't know about winged beasts. It made it a little easier for him to adjust."

Jaycee winced, remembering how he had been placed under Theo's protection and escaped the guy. Theo was sure to be pissed at him. Everyone else was, even if they said they weren't. Jaycee could feel the thick tension in the car. Emotions were running high, and Jaycee was pretty sure they were negative and aimed in his direction.

"Where is Theo, anyway?" Wolf asked.

Jaycee almost smacked the man again when Nazaryth rolled his eyes. Why wouldn't his mate shut up or pass out or something?

"He's at home." Nazaryth sent a pointed look in Jaycee's direction. "Where all mates should be."

Now, it was Jaycee's turn to roll his eyes. "I am not Suzy Homemaker. I have a job, you know. A life." Not that his job was that fantastic, but it was a job. He didn't have much money, but at least he wasn't leeching off of anyone else. There were nights when all he had to eat was macaroni and cheese, but at least he paid for it.

"*Zaterio*, you don't—"

Jaycee's eyebrows shot up when Wolf suddenly snapped his mouth closed, pressing his lips together so tightly that they turned white. He leaned toward Wolf, suddenly less worried about his job and more worried that his mate was in pain.

"Wolf? Are you hurting?"

"I'm fine, *zaterio*."

He didn't sound fine. In fact, Wolf sounded downright pissed off, much like the others in the truck were. Jaycee slumped back in his seat, crossed his arms over his chest, and turned to stare out the window. If Wolf wanted to be upset with him for whatever he had supposedly done, then fuck him.

Jaycee watched as the scenery changed as they drove down the road. Countryside turned into buildings of Brac Village and then faded back into countryside, after a quick stop to let Nazaryth out so he could drive Rico's car back to Pride Pack Valley. After a while, the fields and farms faded away and thick trees took their place.

Jaycee had no idea where they were except that they were headed back to the castle thing his mate lived in, and now, he guessed, he lived in, too. He turned to look at Wolf, smiling when he saw Wolf with his head leaning toward the window, soft snores falling from his lips.

He instead turned his attention to the man in the front of the vehicle. "I assume my place of residence has changed." Somehow, he didn't see Wolf agreeing to him staying in his little house with Rico and his other roommate Mike. The winged beast would probably have a coronary.

"You assumed correctly," Dog replied.

"Then do you think we can stop by my place so I can pick a few things up? As nice as it is to wear Wolf's shirt from time to time, I'd really like to have my own clothes, and my computer." He really needed his laptop. A good shooting game sounded right up his alley at the moment. He had a lot of pent-up aggression that needed an outlet before he clobbered his mate or one of his mate's friends.

"I guess we can do that, but you need to be quick. The faster we get Wolf back to the castle and get him into bed where he can rest, the better."

Oh damn. Jaycee hadn't thought about that. "Maybe we should just head for home. I can get my stuff another day."

"Naw, it's okay, little bro. We can stop long enough for you to grab a bag of clothes."

Jaycee still felt bad, but he really wanted some of his own stuff. He had a bag packed in the car that Nazaryth was driving, but there were a few special items he really wanted to pick up, including a pair of fur-lined handcuffs that belonged to Rico. If Wolf gave him any shit about bed rest, Jaycee was going to use them, and not in the fun way, either.

Chapter Eight

Dog pulled the vehicle over to the side of the road in front of Jaycee's house and turned the engine off. He rested his arms on the steering wheel as he took in the area surrounding the building.

Something was off, but damned if he could figure out what it was. He cautiously cracked the door and then pushed it open. A strong sniff of the night air brought him nothing but the smells that should have been there. Still, he knew something was wrong.

"Jaycee, stay in the car until I check things out." His tone brooked no defiance. He would be doing Wolf and Jaycee a huge disservice if he didn't check things out before allowing Jaycee out of the vehicle. Jaycee may not understand it, but Dog hoped the man listened to him anyway.

Dog scanned the area as he slowly walked up to the front door. The closer he drew to the house, the stronger the feeling grew that something was wrong. Dog knew he was right when he stepped up to the door and noticed that it was slightly ajar. Humans could be stupid when it came to the real dangers in the world, but they usually tried to keep their doors shut this time of night.

Dog edged the door open, his claws extending in case he needed to defend himself, or anyone else. As far as he knew, Jaycee's roommate, Rico, should have been home, but the place was eerily quiet.

Too quiet.

Dog stepped into the house and looked around. Again, nothing seemed to be out of place, but he just had this tingling at the base of his skull that told him not all was as it seemed. Something was definitely off.

Dog started to back out of the house, ready to run back to the vehicle and tell Jaycee that they needed to come back at a later time, preferably with a lot of backup, when he heard a floorboard creak above his head.

Dog froze except to lift his nose into the air and inhale deeply. He could smell human, and the human was injured. The strong scent of blood permeated the air. Dog prayed that it wasn't Jaycee's roommate, Rico. Jaycee would be so upset.

And Dog hated dealing with upset humans.

He crept toward the stairs and then flattened himself against the wall. He drew in a deep breath and then peeked around the corner. The stairway seemed empty. Dog carefully made his way up the stairs, stepping on the edges of each step in case the boards creaked. If there was indeed someone upstairs, Dog didn't want to broadcast his arrival any more than he already had.

Dog had just reached the top of the stairs when he heard a loud scream from outside. It was Jaycee shouting his name. Without another thought, Dog spun around and raced down the steps as fast as his feet would carry him. He jumped the last few steps and raced for the front door. His heart pounded as different scenes of what he might find played out in his head.

But nothing could have prepared him for what he saw the moment he stepped through the doorway. Dog wasn't sure all of his years as a winged beast prepared him for the sight before him.

Wolf lay unconscious on the ground in the middle of the yard. The vehicle they had been traveling in looked like a boulder had crushed it. The cab was crushed in, the windows shattered. Jaycee stood in front of Wolf, waving a large stick back and forth. And right in front of Jaycee was one of the biggest damn hell hounds Dog had ever seen.

Dog instantly launched himself at the hell hound, grabbing him around the throat. Razor-sharp claws dug into his arms as the hound fought him. Dog's powerful momentum carried them past Jaycee and Wolf and right into the side of the vehicle. He shook his head as he lost his grip on the hell hound after crashing into the side of the car. It gave the beast enough time to pull away from him and leap toward Jaycee.

"Oh hell no!" Dog shouted as he jumped after the vicious hound. He was not going to fail his friend's *zaterio*, not after witnessing Jaycee trying to fend off the hound with a stick. Jaycee was terrified. Dog could smell his fear in the air. But the man still stood his ground, defending Wolf. Maybe he needed to reevaluate his opinion of the little human.

And get him a knife.

Jaycee kept trying to hit the hell hound in the head with the stick in his hand. All he was doing was pissing the damn thing off, even if he was doing a pretty darn good job at smacking the beast.

"The mark behind his ear," Dog shouted as he started tearing into the hell hound's back with his claws. "You have to stab him in the mark behind their ear. It's the only way to kill him."

Jaycee stared for a moment and then started stabbing at the hell hound with his stick. Dog would have laughed if he hadn't been in a fight for his life. Stabbing the hell hound with a stick was not going to—damn, it worked.

Dog's eyebrows shot up as Jaycee's stick stuck right into the hell hound's mark and the damn beast dropped to the ground. He stood up slowly and lifted his gaze from the dead hell hound to Wolf's *zaterio*. Jaycee wasn't even paying attention. He had spun around and dropped to his knees, cradling Wolf's head in his lap.

"Fuck me running," he whispered. "He did it."

"Did what?"

* * * *

Jaycee could hear Nazaryth and Dog talking behind him, but he could have cared less what they were talking about. His entire attention was on the unconscious man on the ground. Wolf was still out cold, only now, he had cuts and bruises on him to match his earlier injuries.

From the corner of his eye, Jaycee saw Dog go into the house, but he was too busy worrying about Wolf to ask what the man was doing. Seconds later he was back, talking quietly again with Nazaryth.

Jaycee had never been so scared in his life as he had been when that hell hound attacked them. He had pulled Wolf down further into the seat, hoping that if the hell hound couldn't get to them before Dog returned, they would be okay.

That didn't work so well for him.

The damn hell hound just began crushing the roof of the car. Jaycee had kicked the door open with his feet and dragged Wolf out. He had found the closest weapon he could get his hands on, a stick, and started waving it back and forth like a sword to keep the hell hound at bay.

He had been so scared that Dog wouldn't return in time. But he had. And now the hound was dead. But Wolf still wouldn't wake up. Jaycee so wanted to go somewhere safe and just hide away until this crazy-ass world he was living in started to make sense again. He was just afraid it was too late for that.

He was going to be apeshit crazy for the rest of his life.

"He did what?"

Nazaryth's shout reminded Jaycee that he wasn't alone. There were two men behind him, and they knew more about Wolf than he did. Somehow, that didn't sit well with Jaycee, especially since he didn't know how to properly care for his mate in his condition.

"He won't wake up," Jaycee said as he turned to look at the two men, hoping they had an answer. If Wolf never woke up, Jaycee didn't know what he would do. Being in the winged beasts' world didn't seem quite the same without his mate by his side. "Why won't he wake up?"

"It's okay, *zaterio*," Dog said softly as he walked forward and squatted down next to Jaycee. He quickly checked Wolf over before smiling at Jaycee, which was kind of creepy considering the man never seemed to smile before now. "He is in a healing sleep. It's natural for us. He will awaken when his body has healed enough."

"But—"

"Wolf will be fine, Jaycee. I promise. He just needs to rest."

Jaycee wasn't sure Dog could promise him that the sun would come up in the morning because he was no longer sure it would. If it did, it would probably be purple or something.

"You did good, *zaterio*."

Yep, he was losing his mind.

"How are Rico and Mike?" Jaycee asked.

"Mike?"

Jaycee sighed as he ran his fingers through Wolf's soft hair. "He's my other roommate, but he's never home. He's a workaholic."

"I only found one body, Jaycee."

Jaycee's eyes filled with tears. If Rico were alive, Dog wouldn't have said the word *body*. He wiped his tears on his shirt as he stared down at Wolf, nodding his head as more tears slid down his face. Rico may have been floating along in life, but he was a nice guy. He didn't deserve to die.

"I have to call his mom," Jaycee said. "She needs to know."

"Okay."

Jaycee's head snapped up. "My backpack should still be in the backyard. Can you get it for me?" He had totally forgotten about the thing. Not only were his keys in the bag, but so were his cell phone and his wallet. Dog jogged to the backyard and then came back with Jaycee's backpack. The torn strap sent a chill down Jaycee's spine, reminding him of how all this started. It felt as though that hound had attacked him years ago instead of two days ago.

"Can we go?" he asked. Jaycee did not want to be around when Rico's body was brought out. He wouldn't be able to handle it. He knew he had to call Mike, but he also knew Mike would be at work until later this evening.

"Sure," Dog said as he waved another man over. "This is Damek."

Jaycee nodded, not feeling friendly in the least. His mate was wounded, his roommate was dead, and his world was on its ear. But he did notice that the man had hair so blond it almost looked white.

Jaycee scooted back as Dog and Damek picked Wolf up and carried him over to a truck that Damek and the other guy had driven here. They set Wolf down in the bed. Jaycee jogged over to see thick blankets were laid out in the back, ensuring that Wolf would have a comfortable ride. He hopped into the back and settled next to his mate.

"I'll get the bag the doctor sent with you," Nazaryth said as he walked over to the crushed car and reached inside, pulling the small black bag free. He handed it to Jaycee. "Anything else?"

"Mike needs to be warned." Jaycee told Nazaryth about his other roommate and where he worked.

"I'll make sure he has other living arrangements."

"Can you grab my laptop from my room? It's the one on the left upstairs."

"Done," Nazaryth said and then hit the side of the truck with his hand. Jaycee held on as the truck pulled from the driveway. He stretched out beside Wolf as the truck rocked him slowly back to sleep.

When Jaycee woke, they were inside the hangar. Dog and Damek pulled Wolf from the truck and carried him inside the castle.

"I want to talk to you, Jaycee," Nazaryth said as he walked into the hangar. The guy must have been right behind them. Jaycee looked at the opening to the castle and then back at Nazaryth. He wanted to go with his mate, but the commander had a very serious scowl on his face.

"I want you to tell me how you got out of this castle," Nazaryth said as he leaned against a dusty workbench. It looked as if it hadn't been used in years. Neither did this hangar. There were ten shiny, brand-new motorcycles lining one wall and one Hummer, along with a sports car. Jaycee wanted to drool over the sports car, but didn't think Nazaryth would allow him.

"The plant room."

"The plant room?"

"Yeah, the room with all of the—"

"I know what the plant room is. How did you get out? That entrance is sealed."

Jaycee shook his head. "No, it's not. The big door was right there in front of me. I opened it and walked out," he said. "But I did close it behind me when I left."

Nazaryth cursed up a storm as he opened a panel that had wires sticking out all over the place and punched in some numbers. "I would give you the code, but I don't want you wandering out anytime soon."

When the wall slid back open, Nazaryth pointed toward the entrance. Jaycee rolled his eyes as he walked into the tunnel. He walked up the stairs until he found himself in the living room.

"Don't move," Nazaryth warned. "I'm not sure how that door was visible to you, but it isn't a good thing. No one should be able to enter through here."

Oh, hell. All Jaycee wanted to do was go see Wolf, but another *hell* thing might be lurking around. Jaycee was at his wits' end about those creatures. He wanted to kill them all and be done with them.

His head snapped to the side when someone he didn't recognize walked into the living room. Jaycee grabbed the first thing he found and hurled it at the guy. "Get out!" The small figurine smashed against the wall as the man ducked down.

"That's Trigg. He lives here."

"Oh," Jaycee said. "Sorry."

The man glared at Jaycee as he shook the glass from his shirt. "I didn't know getting a snack was going to be so damn dangerous or I would have brought my knife with me."

Jaycee was trying not to freak out. He really was. But since leaving Brac Village, nothing seemed real. He was surprised he wasn't ranting and raving like a lunatic by now with all the weird and bizarre things going on around him.

Things just seemed to be getting stranger and stranger. But oddly enough, the stranger things were getting, the less freaking out he was doing.

How backwards was that?

Maybe being mated was having an effect on him. Who knew. In this crazy-ass world, nothing was black-and-white. Illogical was logical and crazy was the norm.

Killing the hell hound had probably cured him of his sanity and now he was just as loony as the rest of these men.

"Warn the others, Trigg. The door in the green room was visible to Jaycee," Nazaryth said.

Trigg's lip pulled back into a snarl as he nodded at Nazaryth. "I'll go tell the others," he replied as he quickly walked away.

"I think you need to be introduced to everyone before you shove a stick in them." Nazaryth smirked at him. "I want you with Theo, and this time, don't leave."

Shit. Jaycee had planned on dodging Theo for the next thirty or so years until the shifter wasn't mad at him anymore. He hadn't planned on getting stuck with the guy again.

Nazaryth led him down the hallway of bedrooms until he reached the last door and pushed it open. "Theo, I need you to—"

"Oh, no!" Theo protested loudly. "The last time I had to watch him, the slippery little bastard took off on me. I'm not having Wolf come after me because I lost his mate again."

"I was scared," Jaycee defended himself for the hundredth time. He couldn't seem to catch a break about leaving. He was beginning to wonder if they would hold it against him for the rest of his life, and from what Wolf said, that could be a very long time.

"Then you should have said something and we could have huddled in a damn corner together somewhere. You should have seen how crazy Wolf went when he discovered you were gone."

"Really?" Jaycee asked, a little surprised...and a whole lot pleased by Wolf's reaction.

"No," Theo said. "You will *not* have a pleased look on your face when I talk about Wolf almost handing me my ass." Theo wiggled a finger at Jaycee. "You better look repentant."

"He did not almost hand you your ass," Nazaryth mumbled under his breath.

Jaycee bit back the chuckle.

"Get your skinny ass in here, and if you so much as move one toe out of place, I'm tying you down."

Jaycee looked over at Nazaryth, but the commander just shrugged. "He's the boss."

And here Jaycee thought winged beasts were fierce men.

Pussy.

* * * *

Wolf blinked a few times and then shot up, glancing around the room. It took a second for his surroundings to register. He patted his chest and then his legs, hissing when he hit the injured one. It didn't hurt as badly as it had earlier, but damn if it still didn't throb with pain.

He pushed from the bed, careful about the pressure he applied to his leg. Where was his mate? *"Zaterio, where are you?"*

"Getting the evil eye from a wolf."

It took Wolf a second to figure out that Jaycee was talking about Theo. *"Why, what is going on? Why aren't you with me?"*

"Nazaryth thinks me seeing a door in some green room is a bad thing."

Wolf growled. If Jaycee saw the door in the green room, then someone had gotten in. How? He wasn't sure. Nazaryth had spells and wards all over this mountain. No one should be able to get in.

"You better be lying down, Wolf."

Wolf groaned. Jaycee was playing mother hen, but had no clue how serious the situation was. *"I am."* He hobbled to his bedroom door and cracked it open, peeking into the hallway. It was deathly quiet. The castle was never quiet. Tyson was always sitting on the couch watching a black-and-white movie in surround sound.

Wolf crept from his room, and slowly made his way to Nazaryth's bedroom. He had to check on his *zaterio*, even if Jaycee was about to have a fit. He would weather the man's anger just as long as he could see with his own two eyes that his mate was fine.

"You lived."

Wolf froze when he heard Morbius's voice. How in the hell had he gotten into the castle? It was supposed to be impenetrable. *"Zaterio, warn Theo that the hounds are inside. Tell him to warn Nazaryth."*

"But—"

"Just do it!"

The bond went silent. Wolf hadn't meant to snap at Jaycee, but Wolf needed backup quickly. He was in no shape to fight the hound. "Was it Rythicam who died in the fight in Brac Village?" Wolf asked.

"No," Morbius answered with hatred lacing his words. "It was the other hound and one of the demons. You were supposed to die, not the other way around."

"Sorry I lived."

"You will be."

Wolf leaned against the wall as he laughed. Morbius stared at him like he'd lost his mind, and then the hound snarled. "What's so damn funny, beasty?"

"Them," Wolf said as Nazaryth and the other winged beasts came down the hallway, standing right behind the hound.

"What did you hope to accomplish coming here?" Nazaryth asked. "You should have known we would stop you."

Wolf's blood chilled when a malicious smile formed on Morbius's face, and then he was the one to start laughing. "It is already done."

Nazaryth walked toward the hound until he was nose to nose with the bastard. A low rumbling growl vibrated in his chest as he pulled back his lip in a snarl, his fangs gleaming in the hallway light. "What have you done?" he asked slowly, growling out each word so quietly that Wolf almost didn't catch what the commander was saying.

Morbius smirked at Nazaryth, showing no fear. "Rythicam and I came back to find a way in. I scented a human. I followed his scent and what to my wondrous eyes should appear? A door." Morbius laughed as if he were thoroughly enjoying this. "I came inside and found the human looking around...so I bit him."

"You what!" Nazaryth exploded, backhanding the hound so hard that Morbius spun, slamming into the wall. "Who is he?"

Morbius wiped the side of his mouth with his hand, black blood dotting his skin. Wolf knew how lethal that blood was. The winged beasts wouldn't die from it, but it would be painful as hell if they got any on themselves. Wolf was already in enough pain.

"How the fuck should I know?" Morbius asked. "But I can tell you he stunk like one of your mates."

Wolf's eyes widened when Nazaryth shifted into his winged beast form and went after Morbius, who had shifted into his dog form and taken off down the hallway. The other winged beasts just stood there in shock.

"Whose mate is he?" Trigg asked.

"Find him!" Renato growled. "Search every fucking inch of this castle."

Chapter Nine

Jaycee's head snapped up when Wolf came into Nazaryth's bedroom. He should be mad at his mate for lying to him about being in bed, but he was too damned relieved that Wolf was okay. He found himself running across the room and throwing his arms around Wolf's neck. "I thought something had happened to you."

"It'll take more than a hound to keep me down, *zaterio*," Wolf said as he wrapped an arm around Jaycee. "I'm fine."

"How's your leg?" Jaycee asked as he pulled back, looking down.

"It doesn't feel like someone is sawing it off anymore."

"Then I think I'll go find my mate," Theo said as he hurried toward the door. "A hound I can handle. It's the demons I was quivering in my wolf boots over." Theo stopped at the door, eyeing the pair. "I didn't lose him this time as you can see."

"I see," Wolf replied. "Thanks."

Jaycee hugged Wolf tightly, feeling as if he could breathe again. The man was safe. When he had heard Wolf tell him that there were hounds in the castle, Jaycee thought he was going to lose his mind. He actually tried to wrestle Theo to get to the door.

The wolf won.

"You need to lie down." Jaycee began to pull Wolf toward the door by his hand. "The doctor said a few days' rest, not a few hours'. Plus I need to look at your wound."

Jaycee was thankful as hell that Wolf didn't argue with him. He didn't have the strength to wrestle with the large man. Even injured, he knew Wolf would win. That would only leave the option of hurling things at the guy, and Jaycee couldn't see hurting an injured man.

Not that he wouldn't if it came down to his mate's health.

They made their way down the hallway and back to Wolf's bedroom. "So what happened?" Jaycee asked as they took a few steps at a time. At this rate, they may make it to Wolf's room by sundown. The man was in pain, but was too stubborn to admit it. Jaycee could see the sweat building on Wolf's brows.

"Morbius got in."

"Who is Morbius?"

"He's one of the hounds currently after Theo, and now you, for being a winged beast's mate. He told us that the king decreed all mates are to be killed on sight when found."

Jaycee was getting better at not freaking out, but knowing he had a hit out on him, a hit that couldn't be called off and was being fulfilled by a creature from hell, wasn't exactly a good feeling. It was downright scary. But Jaycee had Wolf to take care of. He would melt down in a corner later.

"Did you kill him?"

"Nazaryth went after him. But Morbius said he followed a mate into the castle, which is impossible since any human who comes near this mountain feels a compulsion to get away as quickly as possible."

Jaycee stopped to turn the doorknob and pushed the bedroom door open. "The spells on the doors make them feel this way?"

Wolf nodded.

"Then where is he?" Jaycee helped Wolf over to the bed and tossed the covers back. Wolf sat down and Jaycee knelt in front of him to unlace his boots. He freed one boot and tossed it aside, working on the other.

"No one knows. The winged beasts are searching the castle for him now."

Jaycee pulled Wolf's other boot off and then stilled when Wolf tucked a finger under his chin and lifted his head. "You look damn good down there, love."

Jaycee swallowed. Wolf's emerald-green eyes had darkened and were currently filled with so much heat that Jaycee felt his cock harden. "N–No sex."

"A blow job isn't too strenuous on my part." Wolf's voice had gone deep, sultry, and Jaycee's heart was pounding as he imagined his lips wrapped around the man's heavy cock. He remembered from the claiming that Wolf's dick wasn't small. In fact, the man had been blessed in the groin department.

He knelt there, staring up into Wolf's eyes as his mate leaned back and unsnapped his pants, his eyes practically pleading with Jaycee not to refuse him. Jaycee should. Wolf needed his rest. He really did. But Jaycee couldn't get his mouth to form the words of protest. He was just as excited about giving Wolf head as Wolf seemed to be about getting it.

Jaycee leaned back, watching Wolf's strong, scarred fingers push past the waistband of his boxers and pull his cock free. It was hard, weeping, and the head was so red that it was starting to turn purple.

Wolf stroked himself a few times, leaning back on one arm. "See, no strain," he said, his voice a bit coarse.

Jaycee nodded without thought as he leaned forward, placing his hands on Wolf's knees. His eyes followed every stroke, watching as Wolf's hand reached the top of his cock, and then his thumb rubbed across the head, the clear liquid smearing until it was a sticky mess.

Jaycee licked his lips.

"Taste it," Wolf encouraged as he lifted his thumb, the pre-cum pulling into a long, unbreakable strand. Jaycee leaned up and swiped his tongue over Wolf's thumb, moaning out loud as the taste hit his tongue.

"Lick the head, Jaycee." Wolf panted. "Clean up my mess."

Jaycee lapped at the spongy head of Wolf's cock, trying to lick every last drop that was smeared across the large, bulbous head. But every time he cleared the mess away, more leaked out.

"Suck the head, baby. Wrap your lips around it."

Jaycee scooted closer, doing exactly as Wolf demanded. Wolf was pushing his erection down toward his mouth, feeding his cock to Jaycee. He suckled with his lips and swiped across the slit with his tongue. Wolf groaned.

Jaycee held on to the cock in his mouth as Wolf maneuvered around, pushing his pants down his legs. Jaycee caught white gauze from the corner of his eye and almost pulled back, until Wolf grabbed the back of his head and held him firmly in place. "Don't stop."

Jaycee heard the desperation in Wolf's voice. He heard the need so clearly that he took the hard shaft a little further into his mouth. The silky skin eased past his lips as Wolf pushed Jaycee's head down just a little further. He pushed back, and Wolf released his head. Jaycee wasn't going to let go, but he wanted to see if Wolf was holding him down or just resting his hand. He liked the idea of Wolf resting his hand.

Reaching down, Jaycee placed Wolf's hand back on his head as he reached between his mate's legs and ran his fingers over the soft sac. Wolf gave a slight push, and Jaycee felt the tip of Wolf's cock touch the back of his throat.

His eyes began to water.

Pulling slightly back, Jaycee concentrated on licking up the hard cock with his tongue, following the heavy vein that ran up the side. When Wolf fisted Jaycee's head and pulled him back, Jaycee chased Wolf's cock with his lips.

"Get naked. I want to suck you at the same time."

"But you can't exert yourself."

Wolf's nostrils flared as he stared down at Jaycee. "Fuck, your lips look so damn good wet and swollen."

Jaycee felt his face flush.

"I'll lie on my back, promise."

Jaycee stood, shedding his clothes and then helping Wolf get his pants off. The man's muscular thighs were a thing of beauty. The lines and dips were so honed that Jaycee wanted to lick every damn golden inch. Wolf pulled his shirt over his head and tossed it aside, scooting back until he was lying in the middle of the bed. "Come straddle my face."

Jaycee's cock throbbed at those words.

Carefully climbing over Wolf's prone body, Jaycee positioned himself over Wolf's head, feeling a tad embarrassed that his cock was dangling over Wolf's mouth. That feeling didn't last long when Wolf grabbed Jaycee's hips and pulled him down, swallowing his cock down his throat.

Jaycee's eyes crossed.

He grabbed the base of Wolf's cock and began to lick the hardened shaft, and then took it into his mouth. Wolf spread his legs wide as he sucked Jaycee's prick like a pro. Jaycee had a hard time concentrating on what he was doing. Wolf was trying to suck his dick from his body.

Wolf tapped Jaycee's hip, and he knew he was neglecting his mate. Using his thumb and index finger, Jaycee pulled at the head of Wolf's cock, widening the slit, and then shoved his tongue inside, wiggling it around. Wolf snapped his hips.

He massaged the underside, where the bundle of nerves rested just below the head, and then swallowed Wolf's cock, parroting every move Wolf made. It wasn't like he had done something like this before, and copying everything Wolf was doing to him helped guide Jaycee.

The sultry sounds vibrating in Wolf's chest encouraged Jaycee to take more, to push a little further. Once he stopped almost gagging, Jaycee took the silky, hard shaft down his throat and then quickly pulled back.

Wolf ran his hands over Jaycee's ass, his fingers playing at Jaycee's hole, and then one lone finger slid inside of him. Jaycee pushed back, desperate to feel more. He groaned around Wolf's cock, and Wolf growled around his. Jaycee grinned. Wolf must really like that. He moaned again and then had to press Wolf's hips down to stop the man from shoving his cock down the back of Jaycee's damn throat.

Found one thing that really turns Wolf on.

Jaycee was rewarded with another finger. He rode Wolf's fingers hard as he hummed and moaned around the man's dick, feeling the building of his orgasm approaching. Jaycee wanted Wolf to come at the same time. He doubled his efforts, sucking hard and fast, pulling at Wolf's balls as he continuously tried to swallow the man whole.

Wolf's fingers bit into Jaycee's side as his hips shot forward, spurts of cum hitting the back of his throat. Jaycee swallowed every last drop. When Wolf shoved a third finger into his ass and started fucking him with those thick digits, Jaycee's body exploded into a thousand pieces as a kaleidoscope of colors filled his vision. Wolf didn't let up. He took Jaycee all the way down his throat, fucking his ass feverishly.

Jaycee rolled from Wolf, landing on his back, his body twitching as he gasped for air. He never knew mutual cock sucking could be so damn fantastic! He wanted to laugh with satiation as his body continued to buzz.

"See," Wolf said as he rested his cheek on Jaycee's calf, "no exertion."

Jaycee smiled as he turned, kissing each ankle on Wolf's legs before he wiggled around until he was in Wolf's strong arms. He loved feeling Wolf's bare, muscular arms wrapped around him.

"*Zymtalium, zaterio.*"

Jaycee lifted his head. "What does that mean?"

Wolf ran his hand over Jaycee's hair and then laid a kiss on his forehead. "I would die one thousand deaths if I ever lost you, mate."

"*Zymtalium*, Wolf," Jaycee replied, seeing the pride and love shine in Wolf's eyes as he repeated the one word.

"*Zymlye*," Wolf said as he pulled Jaycee close. "I love you."

Jaycee swallowed hard, resting his hand on Wolf's chest, feeling his mate's heart beating slowly.

"Z–*Zymlye*, Wolf."

Wolf didn't say a word. He just cuddled with Jaycee until he heard the soft snores rumbling in his mate's chest. Jaycee sighed as he closed his eyes, thankful that Wolf had come after him and brought him home.

* * * *

Renato followed Trigg down to the green room, glancing around every corner and under every planter box, searching for the human who was one of their destined mates. Renato was just as anxious as the other winged beasts to find out exactly whose mate the human was, and dreading the news at the same time.

If Morbius was telling the truth, then the human was lying somewhere, dying from the lethal bite of the hell hound. Renato's stomach was in knots, praying it wasn't his mate. He didn't want that fate placed on any of their heads, but one of the winged beasts was going to go mad when they found this man.

"Anything?" Trigg asked.

Renato shook his head as he brushed aside large leaves on a plant that had grown so large that it was climbing up the wall and he glanced behind it. "I haven't found a clue," he said as he released the plant. It was driving him crazy not knowing who the human belonged to. Every unmated beast was searching in frenzy.

Everyone wanted to know.

Everyone was dreading knowing.

And everyone was preparing to deal with the beast who found out that it was his mate who was either dying or dead. It was a solemn and sobering search, but the human had to be found.

"I found something," Trigg said from the other side of the room. He stood there with his hands on his hips, looking down at the floor, his face grim. Renato wasn't sure what Trigg was staring at, but from the frown on Trigg's face, he wasn't going to like it.

He rounded the table that was holding quite a few of the plants in the room and glanced down, spotting a trail of blood. There were tiny speckles of blood that had splattered to the floor, leading back toward the exit to the outside.

"Do you think it's his?" Trigg asked as he swallowed so loudly that Renato could hear the man's heart beating in his throat. He knew who Trigg was referring to. It could only be the mate's blood. Hell hound blood was black.

"There's only one way to find out," Renato replied. Kneeling on one knee, Renato swiped his finger through the small crimson dot and then licked his finger, tasting the blood on his tongue.

Renato closed his eyes as his entire world came crashing down around him.

He tasted his *zaterio*.

His chosen one.

The other half of his very soul.

Renato stood and let out a heart-wrenching roar, feeling his beast rip its way to the surface as he tasted the noxious taste of hell hound mixed in with his *zaterio*'s life essence. His body jerked and convulsed at the mixture, his chest tightening at what his mate must have gone through at the hands of Morbius.

He staggered back as the tears filled his eyes and then he flew out of the exit, scenting the air around him. He smelled the forest, the humidity in the air, and felt the soft breeze as it slid past him, but he scented nothing that would lead him to his mate.

"What's wrong?" Trigg asked as he ran out of the castle behind Renato, his eyes wide as he snapped his head around.

Renato felt a loss so great encompass him that he dropped to his knees. The hell hound had sentenced him to madness by biting his *zaterio*. He would kill every last one of them if it was the last thing he did before he went mad.

"Is he yours?" Trigg asked gently.

Instead of answering Trigg, Renato shot into the air, searching for his dying mate.

* * * *

Wolf climbed from the bed when he heard shouting. He tucked Jaycee in, his mate still fast asleep, and grabbed his jeans. It took him a moment to wrangle them on, but he managed to get them snapped and then hobbled from his bedroom.

"He flew off," Trigg was shouting. "What the hell are we going to do?"

"What happened?" Wolf asked as he entered the living room.

"The bitten human is Renato's mate," Vydeck answered bleakly. "Renato went nuts and flew off."

Wolf's eyes snapped over to Nazaryth. "And no one is looking for him?"

"Dog and Ruthless went out, and I was just pairing everyone else up, if that's okay with you," Nazaryth snapped.

Wolf knew everyone was under a lot of pressure to not only find Renato, but knowing that the remaining brimstone demon was still out there. He also knew that Nazaryth was spitting nails over the hell hounds breaching their secure castle.

And the commander was feeling the weight of Renato going mad.

"I'm sorry." Wolf bowed his head. "I meant no disrespect."

Nazaryth sighed as he waved Wolf's apology away. "We're all tired. But we have to find Renato. Even if he goes mad, he has to be brought home. I don't want him causing havoc anywhere but here, among us beasts."

The beasts would be able to take down Renato. Wolf winced at the thought of snuffing out Renato's life. Aside from losing one's *zaterio*, madness was the one thing that the beasts worried most about.

"We need to find him," Nazaryth said. "I know he's searching for his mate, but if Renato finds him and he's dead, there's no telling what kind of chaos he can create."

"There's no chance his mate can still be alive," Vydeck said, frowning. "Is there?"

"If he's not dead now, he will be soon." Nazaryth sighed as he rubbed his eyeballs with his fingers. "Humans just can't survive a hell hound's bite."

Wolf crossed his arms over his chest to ward off the chill those words brought him. Jaycee was human. Even though they were mated, Jaycee would still die if he was bitten by a hell hound. And that was something Wolf didn't even want to consider.

"He could be alive," Wolf said, just because he needed to believe that there was a chance for his own mate.

Nazaryth spun around and glared at him. "He's dead!" he shouted. "You know it and I know. In all of our history, no human has survived the bite of a hell hound. It's just not possible."

"It wasn't possible for a human to breach the castle walls either," Wolf snapped right back. "And yet, somehow, Renato's mate did just that."

"Is there any way he could know our ancient spells?" Vydeck asked. "Maybe he counteracted the warding spells Nazaryth placed around the castle."

"Look," Trigg said as he stepped in front of everyone and waved his hand between them in the air, "it doesn't matter how he got into the castle at the moment. We can figure that out later. What does matter is finding Renato and his mate before they both end up dead."

"No, no," Nazaryth said as he rubbed the back of his neck. "You're right. We need to find them both, dead or alive."

"Hopefully alive," Trigg said.

The sad glint in Nazaryth's eyes said he didn't think that was possible. Wolf pretty much knew Nazaryth was right even if he wished things were different. And his heart ached for his friend. He had known Renato for centuries, fought beside him, laughed beside him, and dreamed of having a mate beside the man.

Now, they had both found their mates, only Renato's was dead or dying while Wolf's was lying asleep in his bedroom. While Wolf was overjoyed at the mere presence of his mate, he was heartbroken by the idea that Renato would never feel his joy.

"What can I do to help?"

Chapter Ten

Jaycee's hands shook as he dialed a number on his cell phone and then placed the phone against his ear. This was a phone call he never wanted to make. He and Rico weren't best friends, but they were friends. Jaycee liked the guy.

He didn't deserve to die the way he had.

Hell, no one deserved to die that way except maybe the hell hounds, and the brimstone demons. Jaycee was actually thinking slow torture was good for them. They needed to suffer just like they were making everyone else suffer. That damn king needed it the most.

Jaycee started to growl when he heard a soft female voice answer the phone. He winced and started pulling at a loose thread on his jeans. Gods, he so did not want to talk to Rico's mother.

"Mrs. Cruz, this is Jaycee Raynes, Rico's roommate."

"Oh, hello, Jaycee," the woman replied. Jaycee could hear the sweetness in the woman's voice and knew he was about to crush her world. He felt like he was as evil as one of the hell hounds.

"I have some bad news, Mrs. Cruz."

"Bad news?"

"Rico's been involved in an accident, Mrs. Cruz." Jaycee swallowed back the sob working its way up his throat. "I'm afraid he didn't make it."

Jaycee's eyes nearly popped out of his head when the woman started laughing. He had been under the impression that Rico and his mother were pretty close, especially after the death of Rico's father. Had he been wrong?

"Mrs. Cruz, did you hear what I said?"

"Of course I did, son, but Rico is not dead. He's sitting right here." The woman laughed again like she hadn't just made Jaycee totally speechless. "And he wants to know what you did with his car."

"Uh...I..." Jaycee frowned. "He's sitting right there? Right in front of you?"

"Yes," Mrs. Cruz said. "Would you like to speak to him?"

"Please," Jaycee whispered, holding his breath until he heard Rico's voice in the background. Tears started sliding down his cheeks. Rico was alive. He was...then who was killed by the hell hounds?

"Dude, where's my fucking car?" Rico said when he came on the line. "I was about to call the police and report it stolen."

"It's parked in front of the house," Jaycee said quietly, not quite believing that he was hearing his friend's voice. "Are you okay?"

"I'm fine, dude. Since Mike was working and you had taken off, I decided to go visit Mom for a few days, that's all."

"Good, good, that's a good place to be right now. Maybe you could—" Suddenly, the rest of Rico's words started to make sense to Jaycee, and he knew who had died. "I..." Jaycee swallowed again. "I think Mike is dead."

It was the only explanation.

"What?"

"I think Mike is dead."

"How?" Rico asked.

"There was an attack at the house. When I came home, I found..." Jaycee wasn't sure how to exactly explain this situation to Rico without telling him about the winged beasts and he couldn't do that. "There was a body in one of the bedrooms, but it was beyond recognition. I thought it was you because Mike is always at work and..." Jaycee licked his dry lips.

"Dude."

Jaycee could just see Rico pushing his hand through his dark brown hair, ruffling the ends. It was what the man did every time he was agitated.

"What did the police say?" Rico asked. "Did they catch whoever did it?"

"I don't know. I haven't been back to the house since then and the police haven't come to talk to me." Mostly because they couldn't find him. "I guess they will when the time is right."

"Yeah, yeah. Um…do you think I should come home and talk to them or call them? Maybe they have questions for me."

Jaycee's heart jumped into his throat. "No!"

"Dude!"

"I'm sorry, Rico. I just don't know if they have caught whoever did this and if you come home, they might go after you and…just stay where you are until I call you, okay? I'll give the police your mother's number, and they can contact you if they need to."

Please stay where you are. It was the only way that he could see to keep Rico safe until the hell hounds were killed or stopped coming after him.

"I need my car, Jaycee."

"I'll have someone bring it to you." Who, he didn't have a clue, but maybe one of the winged beasts would drive Rico's car over to him. He could hope anyway. "Just don't come back to the house, not until I give you the all clear."

"Yeah, I hear ya," Rico grumbled. "I'll stay put until you call."

"Thanks, Rico."

"But call me the second you find out if it was Mike or not."

"Yeah, I will." Although, Jaycee was pretty damn sure that it was. "Take care, Rico. I'm really glad you're safe."

"You too, dude." Rico chuckled nervously. "Don't take any candy from strangers."

Yeah, like that was going to happen. Wolf would flip his lid. Jaycee hung up the phone and just stared at it. Rico was alive and

Mike might be dead. He couldn't believe it. He didn't know whether to be grateful or not. He liked Mike just as much as Rico.

This sucked.

"Did you make your phone call, *zaterio?*"

Jaycee glanced up when Wolf walked into the room. He nodded absently. "Yeah, I just got off the phone with Rico."

Wolf's eyebrows shot up. "Rico?"

"Yeah. It seemed he went to visit his mother a few days ago. He's fine."

"So, if that wasn't Rico back at your place, who was it?"

Jaycee sighed deeply. "I'm betting it was Mike, my other roommate."

"Oh, *zaterio*, I am so sorry." Wolf walked over and sat down on the edge of the bed next to Jaycee and wrapped an arm around him.

Jaycee leaned into Wolf, loving the larger man's innate strength. He always felt so safe in Wolf's arms. "I wish I could stay here for the rest of my life," Jaycee mused as he rubbed his cheek against the side of Wolf's chest.

"You can, *zaterio*."

Jaycee chuckled. "Only in my fantasies."

"Where else would you go?"

Jaycee peeked up at Wolf when he felt the man's arms tighten around him. "Well, I have to go back to my place for one, and—"

"The hell you do!" Wolf snapped as he jumped to his feet so fast that Jaycee didn't have time to stop his fall, and fell right into the spot where Wolf had been sitting. He slowly pushed himself up and brushed the hair out of his eyes.

"You're not going anywhere." Wolf snapped his teeth and then pointed to the floor. "This is where you belong, right here with me. Nowhere else."

Jaycee blinked in surprise, and a bit of growing anger. "What I meant was that I wanted to stay wrapped in your arms for the rest of my life. But I knew that couldn't happen because I needed to go back to my house and pack up everything I owned so that I could move in here with you."

Jaycee watched Wolf's face flush. The man's eyes darted away when Jaycee pushed himself to his feet and stepped forward. Jaycee thumped Wolf in the chest with his finger.

"That may change if you think you can control me like some little pet. I refuse to be under someone's thumb for the rest of my life. And mate or no mate, if you ever even think about trying to make me into some little brainless slave, I will become your worst nightmare. You'll wish that you were battling an entire pack of hell hounds by the time I'm done with you."

Jaycee yelped when Wolf's mouth suddenly slammed down on his and the man's arms wrapped around him in a vise grip. Either this was the kiss of death or Wolf was really turned on by Jaycee's little temper tantrum.

The hard cock pressing against Jaycee's abdomen said *horny as hell.*

Jaycee allowed Wolf's tongue to war with his for several moments as his mouth was totally ravaged, and then he pushed away. The puppy dog blinking eyes look Wolf gave him almost did Jaycee in.

Almost.

But he had a point to make.

"Are we clear, Wolf?"

"Yes, *zaterio.*" Jaycee really didn't like the wicked grin that crossed Wolf's lips. "I will continue to keep you safe, making you my prisoner. And you will continue to put me in my place when I step over the line."

Jaycee felt his eyebrows shoot up. That wasn't quite the answer he had been looking for, but it wasn't a bad one either. Jaycee just wasn't sure how to reply to what Wolf had said. If he agreed, Wolf might think that he could walk all over Jaycee. If he remained silent, Wolf might think he didn't want exactly what the glint in Wolf's eyes promised.

"Wolf, I…" Jaycee licked his lips, smirking when Wolf's eyes instantly dropped to his lips and the man's cock pulsed against Jaycee's leg. "Pay attention, beast man."

Wolf's eyes snapped up.

"Your world scares me, Wolf. There are more dangers in it than a Wes Craven horror flick. And I'm not sure how to deal with that. Not even here in your secure castle am I secure. That hell hound got inside. How are you supposed to keep me safe?"

"Remember what I said, *zaterio*. I would die one thousand deaths if I ever lost you."

"Death is still death, Wolf."

"But I will not let you see yours until we are old and grey, and in my world, that could be a very, *very* long time." Wolf reached up and brushed Jaycee's hair back from his eyes, a strange, intense sheen in his eyes. "I will not let anyone take you from me. None of my brothers will let that happen. And even though the castle was breached, Nazaryth is putting in new spells, better spells, to keep us all safe here."

"But—"

"No buts, *zaterio*. You are my world, my very reason for breathing. Keeping you safe is all that matters to me anymore, and I will not let you down. Times may get scary, but as long as we are together, there is nothing and no one that we cannot defeat."

Jaycee felt like the lump in his throat was going to leap right out. He could barely swallow. "Wolf," he croaked out through dry lips.

"*Zymlye,* my wonderful mate."

Jaycee blinked back his tears. "I love you, too, Wolf." And maybe that was all that really mattered.

* * * *

Wolf grumbled as he watched Jaycee practically hyperventilate. He wanted to argue about Jaycee going back to his house, even if the man was packing up all of his belongings to move into the castle.

It wasn't safe.

But after the chewing out he had received when he tried to assert his authority…okay, he had lost his temper, clear and simple, but when Jaycee had mentioned leaving, all he could see was his future without his mate, and he had simply lost it.

Which was another reason he didn't want Jaycee here. But the man had refused to even consider anyone else packing his belongings. He said no one else would know what to pack. And he was probably right. But still…this wasn't the place for Jaycee.

"Are you finished?" Wolf asked as he glanced out of the bedroom window for the hundredth time. He wasn't afraid of a hell hound, not when it was just him. But he had his mate with him and the thought of Jaycee being attacked again chilled him to his very core.

And he didn't even want to think about the damn demon.

"Stop rushing me. If one of those doggies comes back, I'll grab a stick," Jaycee teased as he grabbed a gym bag from his closet. If the situation wasn't so serious, Wolf would have laughed. Okay, maybe not. Nazaryth had told him about Jaycee killing the hound with a damn stick. He still had nightmares about that.

"I'd rather get out of here before they even know we've returned."

Jaycee dropped the bag on the bed and then slapped his hands on his hips, his lips pulled back in a wicked twist. "I've been running from the scary monsters from day one since meeting you. I'm tired of running, and I'm tired of being scared. We can take them," he stated adamantly. "You fly around their heads and I'll beat them with a stick."

"That's your plan?" Wolf asked as he stared in shock at his mate. "I'm still not walking right because of the damn goo that demon spit at me and you want to beat him with a stick?" Had his mate lost his mind?

"Oh, I thought we were talking about the doggies. I didn't know you were referring to the demons." Jaycee cocked his head, tapping his chin with his finger, and then shook his head. "If it's demons, we run like hell."

Wolf did chuckle this time. "I like that plan a lot better."

"Did I ever tell you how handsome you are when you smile?" His mate blushed, his eyes darting around the room as he grabbed some things to pack.

Aw, his mate was so cute when he was shy. "No. But I'm listening."

Jaycee waved a hand at him. "Stop teasing me."

Wolf leaned against the windowsill, his eyes locked onto the yard below. "I'm not teasing you, Jaycee. I like when you give me compliments. It lets me know my *zaterio* wants me."

Wolf glanced at his mate as Jaycee walked around the bed and stopped right in front of him. "Your Cheerio will always want you, Wolf. I may not say it enough, but I think you are the sexiest man to walk the earth, winged beast."

Wolf was the one feeling his face heat up this time at Jaycee's words. His mate's brown eyes were smoldering with lust as he gazed up at Wolf. If only they could fool around, but Wolf didn't want to be caught off guard if something wicked showed up.

"Remind me to thank you later." He winked and then looked out of the bedroom window.

"I can do that," Jaycee said just as his phone rang. His mate snatched his phone from his back pocket and glanced at it. "It's for you."

Wolf frowned when Jaycee handed the phone to him. Who on earth would be calling him on his mate's phone? He glanced at the caller ID and saw that it said *Mom. Oh, hell no!* "It's your mom, Jaycee."

"She probably wants to yell at me for not calling her. Go ahead, big bad winged beast, talk to her." Jaycee opened his dresser drawer and began to pack the gym bag.

Wolf felt his palms begin to sweat as he hit the send button. "Hello?"

"If you weren't my only son, I'd strangle you for ignoring my calls. What the hell has gotten into you, Jaycee? Are you trying to worry your mother?"

Wolf wiped his hand across his sweaty forehead. He didn't have a mother and was clueless on how to deal with an irate one. "This is Wolf, ma'am."

The silence stretched on for so long that Wolf thought the woman hung up. "And who in the hell is Wolf?"

Wolf shot Jaycee a glare, but his mate just hummed and continued to pack as if he didn't see the terrified look crossing Wolf's face at that very second. He was going to make his *zaterio* pay for this. "I'm Jaycee's...*friend*?"

Wolf would never in his life deny his mate, but he wasn't sure what in the hell to say to this woman. Truth be told, she lightweight scared him. He knew his mate loved his mother, and Wolf didn't want to say anything to offend her.

"He's my boyfriend, Mom," Jaycee yelled across the room.

"Oh," Ms. Raynes said, and then Wolf heard a soft giggle. "When am I going to meet my boy's boyfriend?"

Wolf shot a pleading look to his mate, but Jaycee just shrugged. "When can I leave my cage and go visit my mom?" he asked loud enough for his mother to hear. Wolf groaned, slapping his hand on his head as he glanced out of the window.

"It's like that?" Ms. Raynes asked. "Now I know I have to meet you."

He could hear the light teasing in Jaycee's mom's voice, but it did not put him at ease. "I swear there is no cage, Ms. Raynes. Jaycee is just teasing you." And he was going to spank the shit out of his mate for this one. Wolf was so damn embarrassed that he wanted to hang up and go hide somewhere. He had never dealt with a mother before, and was at a loss of what to say.

Jaycee wasn't helping.

She laughed. "Too bad. Just bring my son over this Sunday for the cookout."

Wolf pulled the phone away and stared at it when Jaycee's mom hung up. "Cookout?"

"My family gets together every Sunday for a cookout. I guess you're going."

"But, *zaterio*, it isn't—"

Jaycee held his hand up, stopping Wolf's protest in its tracks. "Then you call Mom back and tell her we're not coming."

"But what if one of the hounds makes an appearance, or worse, the demon?"

Jaycee paled. "I hadn't thought about that. Damn. Mom is going to be pissed if I don't show."

A very small part of Wolf blew out a breath of relief that he wasn't going to have to meet his mate's mother. He dodged that bullet very nicely. He mentally high-fived himself.

"Just have the winged beasts patrol the area."

Bullet, one. Wolf, zero.

* * * *

Nazaryth paced his bedroom, filled with worry over Renato. The winged beasts had no luck finding the man, and by now he knew Renato's mate was surely dead. He just couldn't understand how everything had gone so wrong.

The human shouldn't have been able to breach the wards he had placed on the castle. He should have felt the compulsion to turn around and leave as soon as he entered the nearby forest. Nazaryth knew Renato's mate was human. He had sampled the blood on the floor in the green room. The noxious taste of the hell dweller had also been detected, so there was no doubt in his mind that the human had been bitten.

"You're wearing a hole in the carpet," Theo said as he slid his arms around Nazaryth's waist.

"I'm worried, *zaterio*. Renato will go mad, and we can't find him. If he unleashes his sorrow and pain on the world, people will die. He won't discriminate between a hound and any other person who gets in his way."

"Are you sure he's human?" Theo asked. "Maybe he's a shifter and he's fighting the fever right now like I did."

Nazaryth wanted to believe what his mate was telling him, but he knew better. The blood was human. He had no doubt about that. "No, Theo. As much as I would take comfort in believing Renato's mate stood a chance, I won't allow the lie to take root. He is human."

"Damn, that just sucks," Theo said as he rested his head against Nazaryth's chest. Nazaryth enveloped his mate in his arms, resting his chin on Theo's soft hair.

"I know. I never thought one of my men would suffer this greatly. I always thought we were invincible. Being immortal, I thought we could withstand it all."

"But even being immortal, you can't withstand a broken heart, Nazaryth. There is no way to stop that from happening no matter how invincible you are."

Wasn't that the truth.

"Can't you use your pull as the commander and call him back?" Theo asked as he pulled back slightly and tilted his head back to look up into Nazaryth's face, hope shining in his gorgeous eyes.

"The thought had crossed my mind. But if I open the call up, all winged beasts will hear me, and the king himself as well. If Zephyr knew that Renato was going mad, he would send in a legion of hell hounds and demons to hunt the beast down to kill him. Zephyr would take great joy in watching Renato suffer. I can't risk that."

He was caught between finding Renato, and risking the king's wrath, or remaining silent and praying they found the beast in time. Nazaryth never hated the king more than he did in that very moment. If it took his last breath, he was going to see the king dethroned.

Chapter Eleven

It was Wolf and Silo's turn to patrol the streets of Pride Pack Valley. They had Caymen from Zeus's grey wolf pack with them as well. It was the grey wolves' territory, after all. But Wolf didn't like a shifter patrolling with them.

Not that he had anything against the wolves, but it was too dangerous for anyone but a winged beast to deal with a hell hound. Winged beasts could handle a hound. The shifter only complicated things. Wolf felt as if he were babysitting instead of patrolling.

But Nazaryth and Zeus had decided that the winged beasts needed to show the shifters how to fight the hell hounds. The two leaders wanted the wolves to know how to defend their own territory. They wanted the beasts to show the wolves how to fight without getting bit.

Wolf was still trying to figure that one out himself.

As they walked, Wolf thought about what Nazaryth had told him right before he left for patrol. Dr. Samuel had called and confirmed that the dead body found in Jaycee's house was indeed Mike Baxton, his *zaterio*'s roommate. He knew the hounds hadn't mistaken the human for Jaycee, so the only other explanation was that the hounds were playing with them.

Wolf was not looking forward to telling Jaycee that one of his roommates was dead. He wasn't sure if Jaycee was good friends with Mike, but delivering bad news always sucked.

"So he sent two demons?" Caymen asked as his eyebrows sat high on his forehead. "What do they look like?"

"Like demons," Wolf replied in a deadpan voice. He really didn't want to be out here walking the streets. He knew the patrols needed to stay in place, but there was too much going on for him to be away from his *zaterio*. His mate wasn't safe, and Renato still hadn't been found. He shouldn't be out here walking around. He should be somewhere fighting or looking for the missing beast.

And he missed Jaycee.

"Thanks, jackass," Caymen replied with a slight growl in his voice. "If I want smart-ass answers, I'll go hang around Rave and Taz."

Wolf hadn't a clue who those people were, and didn't care at the moment. He was worried about Renato. He was worried about Jaycee. And he was worried that the hounds would find another way into the castle before Nazaryth finished with the new spells he had found in the Zantharian library he kept in his bedroom.

Hell, he was just plain worried.

Wolf rubbed his thigh, feeling the low throb. He had been cleared by Dr. Samuel to resume his duties, but Wolf hadn't been ready to leave his mate to patrol the streets. His leg was scarred. There was no getting around that. But he was walking without a limp now.

Yee-fucking-ha.

He would have preferred to be limping and lying in his bed with his *zaterio* where he could keep an eye on Jaycee. But Wolf knew it was a joint effort to keep the streets safe for the residents of this town. He was created to kill hounds, so he needed to suck it up and stop complaining to himself about having to patrol.

Wolf had other frightening things to worry about besides what he was already worrying about.

Like meeting Jaycee's mother. Now that thought really did scare him. He had never had a mother. What were mothers like? He was dating her son, after all. Well, he had claimed Jaycee, but as far as she was concerned, they were just dating. From what he had learned about humans, mothers were extremely protective of their offspring.

"Have you guys ever dealt with a mother before?" Wolf asked the two men who were currently discussing the brimstone demons.

Caymen and Silo stopped talking and stared at Wolf strangely. Maybe he should have kept his mouth shut.

"I was created, Wolf. You know that," Silo replied as he scratched his head. "I don't know the first thing about mothers."

"I was taken at an early age by Jackson. I don't remember my mother," Caymen confessed. "Why?"

Wolf wondered if he should even bring it up. In the larger scheme of things, it wasn't something he should be worrying about. She was human. She was a mother. How harmful could she be? Wolf had fought hell hounds, brimstone demons, and a whole slew of other creatures in his lifetime. What was one tiny human to him?

"Never mind."

"No," Silo argued as he stopped walking and turned toward Wolf. "You brought it up. So why are you asking about mothers?"

"Jaycee's mom wants to meet me." Saying that out loud only made his fear of meeting her seem ten times more ridiculous to Wolf. He couldn't believe he had brought it up. She was a human. What was there to be afraid of?

"Did she threaten you to stay away from her son?" Caymen asked.

"No," Wolf said as he shook his head.

"Did she offer to feed you?" Silo asked.

"Yes."

"Then what in the hell is the problem?" Caymen asked. "She didn't threaten to cut off your balls, and she is going to feed you. Stop worrying."

"Unless she plans on poisoning him," Silo muttered to Caymen. "It could happen. I read about that stuff all the time online."

"Man, what in the hell are you reading about that stuff for?" Wolf asked, feeling even more nervous about going to meet Jaycee's mom now. Silo was going to get his ass kicked if he didn't stop planting those seeds in Wolf's head.

He always knew Silo was one strange beast. He was jittery and bouncy, talking as if he had a damn nervous tic or something. But reading about people poisoning others was just downright strange.

And scary.

"I don't think arsenic can kill a winged beast," Caymen replied and then looked between the two. "Can it?"

"I'll go ingest some and let you know," Wolf replied dryly.

"I read about this one case where the mother poisoned her son and his lover, all because she was too chickenshit to admit to her friends that her son was gay. She tried to blame her son's boyfriend, but with today's forensics, they busted her ass."

"Stop!" Wolf growled as he rubbed his temples. "Neither of you are helping me here. You were supposed to tell me it was going to be cool, not scare the holy shit out of me."

"Oh," Silo said. "If you wanted a candy-coated answer, you should have said so."

"It'll be cool," Caymen replied. "Just don't eat or drink anything."

"But it's a cookout," Wolf pointed out.

"You are so screwed," Silo replied.

"You know, Silo, I—" Wolf stopped talking when he scented something strange on the air. He tilted his head back at the same time Silo and Caymen did, all three sniffing.

"What is that smell?" Silo asked.

It smelled like hounds, but there was something strange mingled in with their scent.

"Hounds?" Silo asked.

"No." Caymen shook his head. "Vampire rogues."

The three glanced at each other for a second and then began to follow the scent. "I heard that the hounds had promised the fey to protect them against rogues for something in return. Do you think they're working together?"

That was one scary thought. But Wolf wouldn't put it past the hounds to exploit the vampire rogues and use them to their advantage.

They were from hell, after all. They had no morals. They would use any means available to them to cause havoc and mayhem.

The scent carried them closer to Harold's Deli, but then the smell faded. Wolf stood on the corner of Trenton Street and Route 14 as he glanced around. He scanned the gas station across the street to his right and then looked left to where Pride Pack Valley General was located, but didn't see anything out of place.

It was three in the morning. No one was out. The streetlight on the corner was blinking red, and the wind was blowing by gently, but there were no hell hounds or vampires in sight.

"That's strange," Caymen stated. "The scent just disappeared."

It was strange, and Wolf needed to let Nazaryth know that the hounds and rogues were possibly working together. Or more accurately, the hounds were controlling the rogues now.

Neither idea was pleasant.

* * * *

Jaycee quickly glanced away to keep from laughing when he saw Wolf fidgeting with his collar. It was the third shirt the man had put on, and he found something wrong with each one of them. Wolf was going bonkers. There was no other explanation.

"Wolf, it's a cookout, not the inaugural ball. You look fine."

He really did, and it didn't seem to matter what he wore. He was still gorgeous. Wolf's jeans hugged his legs like a second skin, and they wrapped around his cock like they were made to put the hard length on display.

Jaycee licked his lips as he looked his mate up and down. Oh yeah, the man was totally drool worthy. Besides his skintight jeans, every damn shirt he put on showed off the hard muscles of his chest and abdomen like a wet dream.

"Maybe we should just stay home."

Wolf's head snapped around, a hopeful look on his face. "Really?"

Jaycee sighed, giving up his fantasy of spending the next few hours wrapped in Wolf's arms. "No, sorry, babe. You have to meet my mother or we'll never hear the end of it. But when we get home..." Jaycee watched Wolf's shoulders slump as he let his statement hang in the air. "It's not going to be that bad, Wolf. I promise. If I love you then my mother is going to love you."

"My leg is nearly all better," Wolf said. "I could make it worth your while to stay home."

Jaycee's jaw dropped. "Are you trying to bribe me with sex?"

"Is it working?"

"Uh...no."

"Then it was just a suggestion."

"What would you have done if I had said yes?"

Wolf shrugged. "Stripped you naked, sucked your dick until you screamed my name, and then fucked you into the mattress."

Jaycee gulped. "Oh damn."

"But, since it's more important for us to go visit your mother..." Wolf trailed off as he walked toward the bedroom door. He turned at the doorway and winked at Jaycee over his shoulder. "We should probably get going."

Jaycee stood there in stunned silence as his mate disappeared through the door. He couldn't seem to make his body move for several moments, mostly because his cock was threatening to explode and he was afraid if he moved he would need to change his pants.

He swallowed hard and reached down to thump his hard cock. He winced at the sharp pain and then started for the door. "I may have been a bit hasty."

Wolf's laughter met him as he walked out of the bedroom. "Too late now, *zaterio*. Your mother awaits."

Wolf didn't look quite so amused when they pulled up in front of Jaycee's mother's house thirty minutes later. In fact, he looked downright scared out of his mind. Jaycee wished that there was some way to reassure his mate that everything would be fine, but only time, and meeting Jaycee's mom, would show Wolf that.

"I promise that everything will be fine, Wolf," Jaycee said as he patted his mate's leg. "My mom will love you." Jaycee leaned over to kiss Wolf on the cheek. "I do."

"What exactly happens at these cookout things?"

"Uh…well, there's lots of food, people, and just generally hanging out and catching up on the latest family gossip."

Wolf grimaced as he stared at the house through the front window. "Sounds delightful."

Jaycee laughed. "Haven't you ever been to a cookout?"

"Winged beasts do not have cookouts."

"Too bad." Jaycee opened his door and climbed out of the car. "You have no idea what you're missing."

* * * *

Wolf had a perfect idea of what he was missing…Jaycee naked in his bed. He just hadn't been able to convince his mate that they needed to stay home more than they needed to go to some cookout thingy.

He would have been thrilled at any excuse that could have kept him from attending any function involving Jaycee's mother. It wasn't that he disliked the woman. He had never met her. It was more that she scared him more than a hell hound.

She had the power to take Jaycee away from him. That right there was enough to make Wolf's hands tremble as he reached for the door handle of the car door. He didn't know what he would do if his mate suddenly decided that they didn't belong together.

Dying from a broken heart seemed most likely.

Wolf was terrified. He could barely make his legs work as he climbed from the car and followed Jaycee up the walkway to the house. It took every bit of courage that Wolf had to walk into the house behind Jaycee.

"Mom, I'm home," Jaycee called out.

"I'm in the kitchen, sweetie," an unseen female voice called back from beyond the living room.

"Come on," Jaycee said as he held out his hand.

Wolf gratefully took it just because he needed some sort of physical connection to his mate, and then followed Jaycee through the living room, the dining room, and into what was obviously a kitchen.

Wolf could tell.

A woman that looked like an older version of Jaycee stood in front of a stove, stirring something in a red pot. She looked up when they walked in, a smile crossing her lips.

"Hello, son."

"Mom."

Wolf frowned when Jaycee dropped his hand and walked into his mother's arms, giving the woman a hug and a kiss on the cheek before turning and waving his hand back at Wolf. He preferred it when Jaycee held his hand, especially in this situation. It kept him from feeling like he was going to totally freak out.

"This is my boyfriend, Wolf."

"Mate," Wolf growled and then instantly wished he had kept his mouth shut when the woman's eyebrows shot up. He swallowed hard, not missing the glare his mate sent him, and held his hand out to the woman. "Hello, Ms...uh..."

The woman smiled. "Call me Connie."

"Hello, Connie." God, he so sucked. He couldn't even carry on a regular conversation with the woman. Jaycee was going to strangle him. "Your home is very nice." That was polite, wasn't it?

"Thank you." Connie turned back to the stove and began stirring the stuff in the pot again. "I hope you like homemade macaroni salad."

"Uh, yes?" He had no idea. He didn't remember ever eating it.

Connie laughed lightly. It was a soft lyrical sound, reminding Wolf of Jaycee's laugh. He could see where his mate got it, and the chocolate-brown eyes. Connie's were just a little paler than Jaycee's, as if she had experienced more in life than her son had.

Wolf imagined that she probably had.

"So"—Connie glanced between Jaycee and Wolf—"mate, huh?"

Connie knew about mates? How? Wolf's eyes rounded as he gave Jaycee a sidelong glance of utter disbelief. Jaycee gave Wolf a quick shake of his head, clearly giving Wolf a silent warning to remain quiet.

"That's good," Connie said. "I'm happy for you, son."

"You are?"

Connie smiled at Jaycee. "Of course. Mates have a stronger bond than human couples. I'd much prefer you have a mate than just a human boyfriend. As a paranormal being, and your mate, Wolf will be more invested in your welfare than a mere human. He will take good care of you."

Wolf was too surprised to do more than nod in agreement.

Jaycee, on the other hand, looked like he was about to pass out. "Mom, how do you know about mates and paranormals?"

"Son, I've lived in Pride Pack Valley most of my life. You wouldn't believe some of the things I've seen and heard." Wolf gulped when Connie shook a finger at him. "You all don't hide things quite as well as you think you do."

"Yes, ma'am."

"So." Connie crossed her arms over her chest as she turned and leaned against the edge of the stove. "Just what kind of paranormal are you?"

Wolf shot a glance at Jaycee, unsure if he should tell his *zaterio*'s mom about winged beasts. True, she knew an awful lot for a human, but he wasn't sure if he should pull her further into his world. It was dangerous.

But then again, she would also have the knowledge of exactly what was around her. And knowledge kept a person safe in Wolf's book.

"He's a winged vampire," Jaycee said. "He kills things that crawl out of hell and drinks my blood."

Wolf's eyebrows shot up. "Jaycee!"

Jaycee shrugged, looking wholly unrepentant. "What? It's the truth."

"A winged vampire?" Connie asked as her light brown eyes glanced over Wolf. "I don't see any wings."

Was he really standing in his *zaterio*'s mom's kitchen having this conversation? The woman sure as hell was inquisitive. Wolf wasn't sure if that was a good thing or not.

Jaycee snorted as he leaned into the counter the exact same way his mother was. Their traits and mannerisms were so much alike it was a bit scary. "I said the same thing. Apparently only a winged beast's mate can see them."

"Other winged beasts and hell hounds can see them as well," Wolf pointed out.

"Hell hounds?" Connie asked, her apple-red cheeks paling.

"Come on, Mom. Let me explain to you what you don't know," Jaycee said as he pulled his mom into the living room, leaving Wolf standing there by himself. He glanced into the pot Connie had been stirring and saw baked beans.

Wolf liked baked beans.

"You must be Wolf."

Wolf spun around and saw a man standing there with sandy-blond hair and bright green eyes. "I'm Morgan, Jaycee's cousin. Do you play volleyball?"

Wolf slowly shook his head back and forth, eyeing the man carefully. "No."

"Great, then you're on Donovan's team. We need another player." Morgan waved Wolf toward the door and then walked out.

Didn't he just say he couldn't play? Wolf shrugged and walked out into the backyard. He froze when he saw at least a dozen people, if not more. This was Jaycee's family, and his mate had left him to fend for himself?

Wolf was going to paddle the man's ass later for this.

"Damn, you are one big-ass dude," a guy standing on the other side of a white net said. "I'm Donovan. You're on my team."

Wolf walked around the net and just stood there like everyone else was doing. He wasn't sure how to play the game, but everyone had smiles on their faces. He stilled when the faint smell of blood wafted up to him. He noticed Donovan had a bandage wrapped around his arm.

"How did you get hurt?" Wolf asked as he nodded toward Donovan's injury that still smelled fresh.

"Work," Donovan replied. "You ready to play?"

Wolf nodded, but kept an eye on the man. He wouldn't know if it was the man everyone was looking for without tasting the guy's blood. Wolf was pretty sure Jaycee would frown at Wolf licking his cousin's wound.

"Our serve," Morgan called out and then threw the ball into the air, swatting it with his hand.

Wolf watched the ball drop to the ground at his feet.

"Yes!" Morgan laughed.

"You have to hit the ball back over the net, Wolf," Donovan explained. "You can't let it touch the ground."

Wolf nodded. He could do that.

The next time the ball came his way, Wolf slammed his fist into it and watched as the ball went up into the air...and then over the house.

"A little less forceful next time," Donovan whispered to him. "You want it to hit the ground on their side, not in the next town over."

"No," Morgan shouted, cupping his hand to his mouth. "Let him keep playing that way."

"Don't listen to Morgan," Donovan grumbled.

Wolf noticed Morgan rub at his shoulder, and when his shirt moved, he, too, wore a bandage. What in the hell was going on? Normally Wolf wouldn't have thought anything of it, but it was a large white bandage with speckles of blood on the edges.

"Is your family accident-prone?" Wolf asked as he glanced over at Morgan, who was standing on the other side of the net.

"Something like that."

Wolf wasn't sure what was going on, but he wasn't going to make a stink about it. It could very well be accidents.

But one of them could also be Renato's mate.

Chapter Twelve

Jaycee was pleased as punch. Wolf was driving them home and his mate hadn't stopped smiling. He wasn't sure what had happened in the backyard, but when he had come outside, Wolf and Donovan were yelling *in your face* at Morgan and Francis.

Jaycee had been relieved to find out it was over a volleyball game. Wolf was way too big to start a fight with any of the scrawny people in Jaycee's family.

"I had a nice time," Wolf said as he drove down Route 14. "You have a very nice family."

"*We* have a nice family, Wolf," Jaycee pointed out from the passenger side of the truck.

"We do?"

Jaycee gaped at Wolf and then chuckled at the puzzled look on his mate's face. "We are technically married. That means my family is your family."

"They are?"

The smile on Jaycee's face softened when he saw Wolf's eyes mist. His mate turned away, but not before Jaycee saw the unshed tears. He knew Wolf had no parents, no siblings, not even a cousin or an uncle. He was created, not born, as Wolf had stated a few times. He knew Wolf considered the other beasts his brothers, but Jaycee was more than happy to share his family with Wolf as Wolf had shared his brothers with Jaycee. He was an only child, and to have so many large brothers was a thrill for him.

Maybe he should bring them all over next Sunday.

"Yes," he answered. "You have a mom now, Wolf. Well, she's really your mother-in-law, but you can call her Mom."

Wolf swallowed as he nodded and then cleared his throat. Jaycee wanted to reach over and hug the man, but gave him his moment to compose himself. But it did Jaycee's heart good to see that Wolf was accepting of his family. He wasn't sure what he would have done had Wolf and his family not gotten along. Jaycee's family meant the world to him, and he wanted Wolf to be a part of that world.

"How did your mom take the news about hell hounds and such?"

Jaycee hadn't told Wolf about the conversation he had had with his mom. By the time he joined Wolf outside, the cookout was underway. Wolf had to have eaten half the damn food by himself. His cousins Morgan and Donovan just stood there in awe as Wolf polished off three servings of food.

Jaycee was so damn glad he didn't have to foot the bill to feed his mate. He would have to work two jobs to support the man's bottomless stomach.

"She's glad she now knows about hell hounds. She said she was going to carry a blade with her so she could stab one if they attacked her."

The truck swerved as Wolf slammed on the brakes. When the truck came to a stop, he turned in his seat, his anger hitting the roof. "She is going to do what? You can't let her! I won't let her. The hell hounds would eat her for breakfast! Have you lost your mind?"

Jaycee waited for Wolf to stop yelling before he replied. "I talked her out of it, Wolf. Thanks for the vote of confidence."

Wolf leaned his head into the steering wheel, rocking it back and forth. "I did not mean to yell at you, *zaterio*. But the thought of one of those hounds attacking your mother scares the shit out of me."

"Me, too," Jaycee said as he laid his hand on Wolf's head, rubbing his hand across his mate's hair until Wolf looked at him. Jaycee smiled. "That's why I gave her Nazaryth's cell phone number. I told her to call him if she ever comes across one of them."

Wolf grinned, leaned back, and then laughed. "You did?"

"Well, it was either that or teach her where the mark behind a hound's ear is."

"No!"

"Then she will call Nazaryth."

Wolf pulled the truck back onto the road. "Why didn't you just give her my cell number?"

Jaycee snorted. "Do you really want her calling you? You know she would drill you until the sun came up about everything going on. She plowed into me about how I wasn't freaking out about all of this. Mom thinks you had something to do with my calm demeanor now. I told her I still freaked out, but it was less and less. If she called you, you would never get off of the phone. Would you want that?"

"Yes. I like talking to your mom. She's sweet."

Jaycee grinned. "I knew you two would—" Jaycee's hand slammed into the dash when Wolf hit the brakes once more. "What the hell, Wolf?"

Jaycee glanced out of the windshield and damn near wet his pants. The demon that had been attacking the castle was coming right at them. Wolf cursed and the reversed the truck, driving the truck backward.

"Call Nazaryth!"

Jaycee grabbed his phone and quickly dialed the number, yelling into the phone that the demon was hot on their trail.

"I'm on my way," Nazaryth replied.

"He's on his way," Jaycee said as he tossed the phone aside. "Faster, Wolf, faster!" The demon was so close that Jaycee could see the spit that drizzled out the side of the damn thing's mouth. Wolf had told him about the spit, and Jaycee had no intentions of having any of that goo on him.

"He's spitting!" Jaycee shouted as he watched the demon rear its head back and open its mouth. The sharp row of teeth wasn't comforting.

"Hang on!" Wolf cut the wheel so hard that the truck nearly rolled, but they dodged the acidic goo.

Jaycee was never more thankful when he saw the winged beasts heading his way. There were ten of them, all flying close. The demon turned and began to spit at the men approaching.

"He's not following us anymore."

Wolf turned around to look out of the windshield and then stopped the truck. "Stay here, *zaterio*. That bastard is going back to hell."

Jaycee nodded quickly and then reached over and locked the door when Wolf got out. He may have killed a hell hound, but Jaycee knew that was sheer luck. The demon was ten feet tall. There was no way a stick would work on the thing.

The beasts fought the thing, stabbing at his head and dodging the acidic missiles. That was just gross. Whoever created those demons needed to be smacked. Spitting was just nasty. Jaycee gasped and nearly climbed onto the dashboard when he saw Renato fly in, helping the winged beasts take the demon down.

It hadn't been easy by the looks of the fight, but the demon finally lay on the ground, presumably dead.

Dead was good.

For an acid spitting demon, dead was perfect.

As Wolf hurried back toward the truck, Jaycee watched Renato take off again. Only this time a few of the winged vampires followed him.

The truck door opened and Wolf climbed in, wincing.

"Did you get spit on again?" Jaycee asked as he began to pull at Wolf's clothes, checking for any signs of damage. His heart was racing out of control. He remembered what that stuff did to Wolf's leg. It was still scarred badly, but Wolf was finally walking normal again.

Or damn close to normal.

"No, *zaterio*. I didn't get spit on, but Trigg flew right into my damn leg." Wolf rubbed his leg with both hands and then pulled the truck onto the road.

"You're just going to leave that thing in the middle of the road?" Jaycee asked as he glanced behind them. The demon was still on the ground thankfully, but the winged beasts were gathering around it.

"No, he has to be burned in order not to rise again. The others will take his body away before anyone sees it and burn him."

Jaycee really didn't want to know.

"What about Renato? I saw him come to help."

Wolf nodded. "He did. The others are going after him now to bring him home."

Jaycee could hear the worry in Wolf's voice. It made his heart hurt to see the sadness in Wolf's emerald-green eyes. "And?"

Wolf blew out a long breath as he glanced over at Jaycee. "And when he goes mad, it will be his brothers who take his life."

That was a burden Jaycee never wanted to carry. It was a burden he didn't want Wolf to carry either.

It seemed that the crazy world he now found himself submerged in wasn't going to get saner. But as long as he had Wolf, Jaycee was willing to become one of the certifiable.

At least his life wasn't boring.

But a little less frantic would be nice.

* * * *

Not wanting to spoil the cookout Jaycee and Wolf had attended at Connie's house, Wolf had waited to tell his mate about the dead body at Jaycee's.

As far as telling Jaycee that the dead body was Mike, Wolf was glad Jaycee didn't go apeshit. His mate had shed tears though. Wolf hated to see his mate cry when there wasn't a damn thing he could do. He felt so helpless.

But his mate was resilient. Jaycee mourned the loss and swore he was going to arm himself with a collection of sticks. The man was truly trying to give Wolf a coronary.

Wolf watched Jaycee move around the room as he finished unpacking his belongings. His cock was getting rock hard just watching the way Jaycee's ass moved back and forth. The man had a way about him that drove Wolf crazy. He couldn't seem to get enough of his *zaterio*'s body.

"Are you going to watch me the whole time?" Jaycee asked as he shoved his shirts into one of the drawers.

"I had planned on it," Wolf replied as he lay across the bed on his stomach, admiring the view. And it was such a nice view of Jaycee's ass. He was getting even harder as his mate bent over to store something in the bottom drawer. Wolf could feel his erection pressing into the mattress, and he wished it was Jaycee's ass he was pressing it into.

"You know I'll have to find work since my dickhead boss fired me for getting attacked and kidnapped," Jaycee commented as he closed the dresser drawer and then straightened.

"You told him that?" Wolf asked in shock.

"No, but I told him I had a family emergency that took me away for a few days. He said it was considered a no-call, no-show, so he fired me. I wonder who else is hiring around town. Of course, I'll need my car, but that hunk of junk is still curbside."

Wolf growled as he rolled from the bed. "You cannot work, Jaycee. It is too dangerous for you to be out there by yourself. What if a hound finds you, or a rogue? It isn't safe, *zaterio*."

"So, what, you want me to sponge off of you?"

"It isn't sponging if we are mates, Jaycee." Wolf pulled Jaycee back toward the bed, wanting to forget the conversation about finances and fuck the man until they were both limping.

"Are you trying to distract me with sex this time?" Jaycee asked as a blush brightened his cheeks.

"Maybe." Wolf grinned. "Is it working?"

"What were we talking about?" Jaycee laughed gently, his rich, chocolate-brown eyes filled with a humor and tenderness Wolf never wanted to lose. The man was amazing, simply gorgeous, and the perfect mate for him.

"We were talking about me giving you a blow job."

Jaycee's eyes widened in surprise. "We were?"

"We were," Wolf agreed as he deposited his mate onto the bed and yanked his jeans free. The delicious cock that he now craved bounced free, and Wolf didn't hesitate to drop to his knees and swallow the beautiful length in one smooth motion, sucking hard and ferociously.

"Oh!" Jaycee yelped. His hands landed on Wolf's head, his legs spreading wide apart. "Hell, yeah!"

Wolf chuckled around his mate's length and then began to gently roll Jaycee's sac around in the palm of his hand as one finger circled his mate's tight entrance.

"Grab the lube"—Jaycee panted—"if you're going to be playing back there."

Without releasing his mate's shaft, Wolf stretched his arm over to the nightstand and grabbed it. He could feel the pulsing of Jaycee's cock in his mouth as he wet his fingers and then he wiggled them inside his mate's ass.

"Just like that, Wolf. Just like that!"

Wolf pulled all the way back out and then pushed back in, fucking Jaycee with his fingers for a few strokes as he bobbed his head over his mate's cock.

"Wolf!" Jaycee shouted as hot spurts of cum shot down his throat. Jaycee clamped his hands down on Wolf's head and pumped his hips toward Wolf's mouth, fucking it in frenzy.

When Wolf pulled back, Jaycee released him.

"Good gods, man. Where did you learn how to do that?" Jaycee panted as his wobbly legs fell to the sides. "My turn."

Wolf stood, released his cock, and started stroking himself quickly. "I'm already too damn close. Just open wide."

Seeing Jaycee lying there with his mouth wide open for Wolf sent him over the edge quicker than anything in his life. Wolf leaned forward as he growled, pearly-white ropes of cum shooting from the head of his cock and landing on Jaycee's chest and neck. There was a small splatter on his chin.

"I think your aim is off."

Wolf leaned forward, taking in a shaky breath, and then grinned. "But you look damn good wearing my seed, Cheerio."

Jaycee ran his fingers through Wolf's spunk and then licked his fingers. It was the most erotic thing Wolf had ever seen. He wanted to paint Jaycee's entire body and mark him so everyone in the world would know the man was his.

That, and Jaycee looked sexy as hell lying there with spunk all over him.

"*Zymlye*, Wolf."

"You are learning, mate." Wolf grinned as he helped Jaycee to his feet and then smacked his ass. "Keep this up and you will be speaking Zantharian in no time."

"Really?"

"No." Wolf chuckled when Jaycee gave a small growl and smacked his arm. "But over time, I will teach you to speak our tongue. You sound sexy when you speak Zantharian."

"It sounds exotic."

"It is a very exotic language," Wolf said as he led his mate to the bathroom. "And soon you will be speaking it in bed."

"You're going to teach me all the naughty words first, aren't you?" Jaycee asked as he reached into the shower and cut the water on, a pretty pink blush chasing across Jaycee's cheeks.

"You're damn right," he replied. He wasn't stupid. Of course he was going to have Jaycee shouting out his pleasure in Wolf's native language. Was there anything sexier?

"I need to go talk to Nazaryth while you shower." Wolf turned to leave, but Jaycee grabbed his arm.

"It's about my cousins, isn't it? I saw the bandages on both Morgan and Donovan. Do you think they were here?" Jaycee sounded worried, and Wolf couldn't blame the man. If it truly was one of his cousins, then the man needed to be brought here before a hound finished the job.

Wolf cupped the side of his mate's face. "I'm not sure what's going on with them, but if one of them was here, then Renato has a right to know."

"But they're human!" Jaycee said. "How can they survive a bite? I was just scratched, and it hurt like a bitch. You told me a human couldn't survive a bite. It can't be either of them."

Wolf didn't think a human could either. In all the years he was alive, he had never heard of a human surviving a hell hound bite. It was impossible, but he just couldn't shake the gut feeling that one of them had been in the green room. It was like a gnawing feeling in the pit of his stomach.

"They can't, but I would rather rule them out than forget about what I saw and then have a hound go after them."

"No!" Jaycee shouted as he grabbed Wolf's arm and shook it. "They're my cousins. You can't let anything happen to them."

Wolf gave a quick, grim nod. "Then let me go to Nazaryth and tell him what I suspect. It may not pan out to be anything, *zaterio*, but we have to look into it."

"Go," Jaycee said as he pushed Wolf from the bathroom. "Go find out if they're okay. Call Mom."

Hearing Jaycee refer to Connie as Wolf's mother made his stomach flutter. He had a mom. Something Wolf never thought to have. Jaycee just didn't know how much that meant to Wolf. He would be forever grateful to his mate for giving him not only a *zaterio*, but a family to call his own.

He had the winged beasts, but having Jaycee's family was different. They interacted with him differently and treated him like one of their own. None of them were warriors, yet Wolf had felt an inherent strength in all of them. He could tell they loved their cookouts, and it meant a lot to them to be gathered together as a family.

He couldn't wait until next Sunday.

"Thank you, *zaterio*." Wolf kissed each side of Jaycee's mouth and then his lips. It was tender and just a small kiss, but Wolf poured his emotions into the brief touching of their lips.

"For what?" Jaycee asked as his hands pressed over Wolf's, looking up at Wolf as if the sun rose and set for Jaycee in Wolf's arms. He liked that look.

"For giving me so much," he replied.

Jaycee's smile curved with tenderness. "I'm glad you came after me, Wolf. I can't imagine my life without you in it, even if it's filled with monsters."

"What, are you afraid of monsters now?" he teased.

"Hell yeah." He snorted and then changed the subject so quickly that it took a second for Wolf to catch on to what his mate was saying. "I was thinking about having the winged vampires over next Sunday."

It didn't take him long to catch on, though. Wolf growled. "All of them?" Connie would flip. Wolf could just see her questioning each and every one of them about the hell hounds. But then again, she was a great woman to have as a mother-in-law. He knew the winged beasts would love her just as much as he had grown to love her. She was a wonderful person, and Wolf loved her just for giving birth to Jaycee.

"Yes, Wolf, all of them. Go talk to Nazaryth and let me know what he says," Jaycee said as he stepped into the shower.

"I will." Wolf left Jaycee to go find Nazaryth. He had to tell him about Jaycee's cousins and find out which one might possibly be Renato's missing mate. He knew it was impossible. Wolf knew it was crazy. No human could survive the noxious poison in a hell hound's bite.

But he couldn't shake that feeling.

And if one of them were Renato's mate, it would save not only Renato from going mad, but it would take the burden off of their shoulders of having to kill the beast.

And that was worth it to Wolf.

Renato was their brother, with them for more years than Wolf could count. And killing the beast was something Wolf wanted to avoid at all costs.

He glanced back at the bathroom, smiling as he heard the shower turn on. For two thousand years Wolf had been alone, no mate at his side. Even with Jaycee running scared in the beginning, Wolf knew everything they had been through, and things still to come, were all worth it as long as he had his Cheerio at his side.

* * * *

Renato sat on the cliff's edge, staring over the countryside and feeling a loss so profound, so unimaginable that he wasn't sure why he hadn't gone mad yet. His mate was surely dead by now. It had been a week since discovering the blood in the green room.

A human couldn't survive a bite.

His heart had died with his mate, and Renato knew the madness would come soon. There was no way it couldn't. His *zaterio* had died alone, without his winged beast at his side. Renato would never forgive himself for not finding the man in time. It was a pain so raw, so encompassing that Renato stared over the cliff's edge, yearning to join his mate.

He heard the footsteps approaching from behind him and knew that it was the commander. Renato didn't want to hear anything the man had to say. What was there to say? His *zaterio* was dead, and Renato couldn't find it in his heart to care about anything anymore.

"We need to talk, Renato," Nazaryth said as he squatted down at Renato's side. "I think your mate is still alive."

THE END

ABOUT THE AUTHOR

Lynn Hagen loves writing about the somewhat flawed, but lovable. She also loves a hero who can see past all the rough edges to find the shining diamond of a beautiful heart.

You can find her on any given day curled up with her laptop and a cup of hot java, letting the next set of characters tell their story.

For all titles by Lynn Hagen, please visit
www.bookstrand.com/lynn-hagen

Siren Publishing, Inc.
www.SirenPublishing.com

CPSIA information can be obtained
at www.ICGtesting.com
Printed in the USA
LVOW04s1206210516

489338LV00013B/266/P

9 781622 420988